On the Wide African Plain

On the Wide African Plain

And Other Stories of Africa

Rick Fordyce

Merrimack Media
Boston, Massachusetts

Library of Congress Control Number: 2016906899

ISBN: print: 978-1-945756-00-9
ISBN: ebook: 978-1-945756-01-6

Cover photo credit: Rick Fordyce

Published by Merrimack Media, Boston, Massachusetts

This book is a work of fiction.

An earlier version of *Away*
originally appeared in *Crab Creek Review*

To the writers of fiction

Contents

Also by Rick Fordyce

Glen
a novel

I Climbed Mt. Rainier with
Jimi Hendrix's High School Counselor
and Other Stories of the Pacific Northwest

Away

ONE

The man arose from his bed in the early morning light and walked out onto the porch of the small cement house in the clearing beside the road just out of the village, and, looking onto the potholed, tarmac road, watched as a barefooted African woman came up from the village with a large basket of farming cutlasses balanced on her head; and the man knew the woman would try and catch a glimpse of him standing on the porch and watched as she twisted her eyes to the side, but without stopping or slowing her quick pace, or trying to turn her head; and then she was down the road and around the bend.

The man walked down the porch to the small room off the end that was called the kitchen and went inside. There was an old sheet of plywood that was the kitchen table and took up fully a third of the small room and on the plywood there were several plastic containers; some with food: one with rice and one with sugar, and two more that were empty. And beside the plastic containers were some cooking utensils and dishes and a small kerosene-stove, and next to the stove in a small plastic bowl was an egg.

Maybe there will be some bread in the village this morning, he thought, and I can eat it with the egg. The egg has been there on the table now for four days, but I can't cook it to eat without some bread to eat with it, so I hope they will have some this morning like they said last night they would. Then I can drink hot coffee, too, and with the rest of the milk sucree´, and it will be like having a real breakfast.

The man walked out to the road and down the short distance to the cement and mud-brick-house village where, on each side of the dirt main street, village women were setting up hot morning foods to sell on low tables; and the many children held their brightly-patterned *Adrinka* cloths up high over their shoulders in the cool morning air and there were many goats running about, as many as children it seemed. He walked swiftly past the large pots of steaming rice and beans, and the small chips of cassava boiling in thick palm oil; and it was early enough in the morning so that no one called out to him like they would do later after they had eaten and were more awake and the damp air became hot.

At the house where the bread was made on a side street away from the center of the village, he stopped and entered through the wood front door, and, sitting just inside on the cement floor was the first child, young; and the child called out excitedly the man's name for the rest in the house to hear and then taking the man by the hand, led him into the small central courtyard of the compound where the women came shyly out from side rooms covering their breasts with their large day-cloths; and in the courtyard there were many more children. Then, entering with a strong air of authority, in came the head-mother and told the man that she was sorry but today there was no bread. She told the man about the bread and he turned and walked back to the main door; and the children crowded closely around and pushed and shoved to be nearest and then gathered in the doorway and watched as he went up the dirt road.

Back on the main street in the rapidly warming day, he stopped at a small table and bought a few shelled peanuts that were wadded up in a scrap of paper, and, putting them into his cloth shoulder-bag, went back up the road to the house and into the kitchen and began to boil water for coffee. Sitting at the plywood table, he drank the cup of hot instant coffee sweetened with the milk sucreé and ate the freshly roasted peanuts and looked again at the egg.

They should have bread today at the school, he thought, and then I can bring some home to have with the egg for breakfast tomorrow. And if the school bus goes to Tarkwa on Friday I will have the driver bring back some chocolate. No, I will go and buy the chocolate myself, and then I can stop in at Kobina's Food Bar for rice and lamb, and maybe they will have beer. If they don't, I can still take the afternoon bus to Oboso and get off at the club at the bottle factory and maybe get a beer there if the managers are drinking, maybe.

The man went into his room off the porch and took from his desk the books that he would need for the day's teaching at the small secondary school in the clearing down the road from the house, and, closing the room door behind him, walked out to the road and down the road to the school.

Later, in the afternoon heat, he came back up the road to the house and before turning into the yard stopped and looked back down the road toward the school for the student who each day brought his mid-afternoon meal from the school kitchen; but the student was no where to be seen and so crossing the yard and entering his room, he changed out of his teaching clothes, now soaked with sweat from the walk home in the hot afternoon sun, and into a pair of denim shorts and a fresh, light shirt. He then sank into the soft chair in the corner of the room and looked out through the open windows to the forest-covered hills, and, coming up big through the dense lush green, the tall stark-white trunks of the massive hardwood trees; and he could faintly see the movement of their highest branches in the afternoon breeze and the heat waves rising into the air off the distant tops.

The magazines did not come, he thought; maybe they will come tomorrow. But, no, who cares what the president is trying to get done now, or even what the good movies were back home last summer. But in the last magazine it said there were some big ones coming out and everyone was going out to see them. Well, I can see them all when I go back, they should come around again sometime. Maybe one will even come to Accra. That would be good. But it doesn't matter, in December, when the schools have vacated for Christmas, Jim and I can go up north, maybe all the way to Bamako, at least up to Bolga, and it will be the cool season then in the north and at night it will get cold. That will be the best: cold, and dry. And we might even see some game, there is supposed to be some above Bolga.

The boy came from the school with the man's meal and placed it on the table in the kitchen and then went into the man's room and asked about the part of the math lesson that had come near the end of class; and he told the man that it was very difficult but that at home in the evening after the small brothers and sisters were asleep on their cloths on the floor he would try and work the problems, but they were very hard. Then he left and went back out to the porch.

Why haven't the football statistics come yet, the man wondered, alone again in the room on the soft chair in the heat of the late afternoon. I wrote to

Dad over a month ago to send them. It was very clear that I wanted the weekly log with the scores to date. The playoffs start in a few weeks and I don't know anything after the third week.

A light breeze came into the room and blew a sheet of paper off the desk and onto the cement floor.

And I wonder what Kay is doing now, he thought, still in the chair, now looking at the sheet of paper at his feet. She must be through with the program at Indiana by now. She should be wherever it is she got accepted out west; but she didn't know where she was going to be. Maybe Oregon, that would be good, then she could be near Mother and Father for a while.

He got up from the chair and put the paper into the desk and went out to the porch and down to the kitchen. His meal was waiting in covered pots on the table, and, removing the lids, he dished out the steaming rice and hot fish stew cooked in palm oil onto a plate. He then sat down and ate the meal, including a small piece of bread that had come from the school. Then he took a piece of chocolate from a small plastic container and ate it.

Maybe they'll have beer tomorrow at the bottle factory, he thought at the table in the kitchen. Afful said he'd go to Tarkwa with the school bus, too, and then to the bottle factory with me. Or maybe there will be some at Salomey's mother's bar. And then I could buy hot kebobs across the street for a cedi each and bring them back to the bar and eat them while I drink the beer. Those ones would have plenty of the hot pepper, too, like the last time. And the man will remember me and give me good ones and they'll burn bad going down but the beer will wash it away. The man will remember me all right; they always remember me because I am so white: too white; too white for anything. But Solomey's mother will have eggs, too, and I can get bread at the bus stop at the edge of town and maybe in the government store there will be marmalade. That would be the best: I could fry eggs and eat them with bread and marmalade both mornings this weekend. And if there is cow meat to buy, too, I can cook it to eat on Saturday after the students have come for tutoring. That would be good to do.

He got up from the table and washed his hands in the plastic water bowl in the sink and then went out to the porch while his boy, the student, washed the pots and plates from the late afternoon lunch. Out on the road in front of the house, the men from the village were returning from the valley farms as the sun began to set and the shadows of the palms and tall hardwood trees cast longer across the tarmac road. Two men, balancing large bundles of sugarcane on their heads, came up the road and stopped in front of the house, where an older farmer had the strong, smooth palm wine, fresh from the forest; and the two men set the bundles on the side of the road and began to drink the wine. Soon another farmer came up and began to drink, too. Then together they turned and looked at the man standing on the porch and called out to him in the local dialect to come and drink the palm wine with them. They called him by his African name because everyone in the area knew he was there and they all knew his African name; and the men told him to come and drink the sweet wine with them. But the teaching man told them no: he said, no, but thank you, in the local language. They laughed hard when he said no to them in the local language; they liked him for saying a local word, and they drank some more. Then the old one with the palm wine took from his ragged shoulder bag a thick wad of the strong, locally-grown hemp and rolled a large cigarette and the four of them smoked it together, and, talking loudly and more rapidly in the local dialect, drank down more of the smooth wine. Then they picked up their belongings and headed down the road toward the village as they continued their loud and fast conversation. Back on the porch, the man got a strong whiff of the hemp smoke that had drifted over from the road, and, as he looked out across the darkening valley toward the hills on the horizon, a scene came into his mind of riding in the back seats of old cars on dark rainy nights as a youth in the city where he had been raised. Then the scene quickly disappeared as the boy came out of the kitchen with the plates and pots from the afternoon meal, and the man walked down the porch and entered his room and sat again in the soft chair.

Maybe I should go to Accra in February and take the Foreign Service Exam, he thought in the chair, looking again at the distant hills, darkening rapidly with the setting sun. Maybe it would be a good thing to do. What else will I do when my two years are over here and I go back? Go back to school? No. But maybe. Maybe go to some kind of graduate school for a more technical degree, and then come back and work on a development project and get paid real money. But, no; I can't see it. I can't see coming back to work here; alone, anyway. But it might pay money. And then during the summers I can go back to East Africa, back to the coast, and stay there and rest and eat the hot sambusas with beer and swim in the warm ocean; and at night in the big towns on the coast I could sit in the open-air cafes and drink coffee and watch the *Somalis* go by with their baskets of spices. But it is too hot here in this place, that's for sure, and there is not enough to eat. But back home what can I do? Labor? No, I can't do labor again. It would kill me. It would kill my heart, anyway. Maybe teach or go back to school and get a teaching degree and go off and do that. But it is just not the same with work back home now; maybe some kinds, but not the ones I know. You can be from there, even the good parts of the middle class, and live there, but you can't be happy like when you had money because you can't get a job to get money because you don't have the skills. You have to have skills, they say, but you have to buy them with your life, and you don't have the money to even do that. But it is the same for all of the young middle class there, isn't it? All the white class?

To stay here in this place I think I might die, before I should die. Here it is so far away from anyplace. No, I should go back home and start again, like these other Americans who come here for some time and then go back and live and work in America again; but not in the suburbs, that would be too difficult. But it can be hard to leave here because you come to this place and it is very alive here, you can sometimes feel very alive: Like when the bus comes down from the north and the *Mossi* get off at the market with the big bundles of the good smocks and the people want the smocks but they can't get them because the *Mossi* are taking them down to the coast, except for the ones they'll leave in the shrine down a ways. It is very alive here then, and if it is the late afternoon when the pito beer is flowing strong in the streets and you are there when the bus comes in from the north, then it is the best place to be in all the world; better even than back home. But if it is in April or March it is too hot, and in the afternoon if you have to go into town the older children will laugh at you; they'll laugh at you hard. And they will not let you alone because it is their town and you are too white; but they like you a lot anyway. But they will not let you alone, not until you are back in your house and in your room and a student from the school makes them go away. They are just very curious, though. They see that you have come and that you are very different, and they do not see others that are different, and you are very white and they like the light color. They pray that they will have children who are light colored; but not white, that is too light, nothing should be so white, not even the yam dough when it is pounded in the morning, it should have some color too; but they like you very much anyway even though the great tree-god made you so white.

But I should try and think about what I will do next year when I go back home, he thought, and not daydream. I will have to get a job and work somewhere; unless I decide to stay here and not go back. But it is too hard staying here for more than two years, I won't last after that. The Peace Corps is glad I am here, though; they tell me they're glad. But I'll have to go back. Maybe to graduate school. Maybe there is a list of graduate schools that I can write for and then I can pick a good one to go to. But in what? I don't know now, but I'll write for the list before I leave for the north.

Out on the road, the last of the farmers were making their way back to the village as the sun began now to go down fast. The boy from the school who brought the man his meals came up with a bucket of bath water from the small stream down the road and set it on the cement floor of the bathing room that was off the porch across from the kitchen. He then left again for the school to wait for the evening meal to be made to bring to his teacher in the small, cement house.

In his room, the man undressed, and, wrapping a fresh towel around himself, went out to the porch and down to the bathing room. Removing the towel and squatting beside the large bucket, he splashed the cool stream water onto his salt-parched skin and then scrubbed long and hard with the bar of fragrant soap. He splashed more of the water onto himself then, picking the bucket up into the air, poured the last of the water over his head and felt the coolness of the early evening air on his wet body. Drying himself with the towel and wrapping it back around, he walked barefoot across the cool cement floor of the porch to his room. The sun was down now behind the hills and, in the darkness of the small room, he struck a match and lit the kerosene lantern which cast his shadow large onto the wall. Outside in the early evening the fireflies began to appear, sparking quickly through the warm night air, and the crickets began to squeak, many of them and loudly. In his room, the man held the lantern up high and looked over the walls for mosquitoes. He did not want to have to deal with them this evening.

I'll try and kill every mosquito that I see, he thought. They are trying to kill me and so I'll kill them back; worse. So far I've been lucky. They haven't killed me bad, but they've killed me a lot.

He looked at the dark mosquito net hanging over his bed.

One got in there last night, he thought, and I could hear him loud around my face, but I couldn't kill him. Once they get in there all you can do is go under the sheet and hope they don't get you too bad, because you can't ever get them when they are moving about.

He held the lantern up close to a wall and looked carefully some more for mosquitoes. He didn't see any.

You can kill them on the walls, though, he thought. I wish to hell they wouldn't come in here at all, but they are so hard to kill. Even with all the screens up they still get in. It must be that they come in when people come through the door. They aren't so bad during the day but at night they will drive you to a place you don't want to be. And they will eat your damn blood and then in the sun the next day you have to try to keep the damn flies off the bite and you can never do that if you are out in the hot sun waiting for a bus and you have to wait several hours and it is hot. It is no wonder that no one likes it here when there is no beer, or the smooth wine from the palm trees, and you have to know that the mosquitoes liked to kill you and it is hot and the bus won't come and you are carrying a lot and can't reach down to scratch it. The people need the beer, but the government won't give the ingredients so that it can get made, so we all have to go with the cassava that ferments badly but strongly and then burns going down, and makes you nauseous later on; and makes some of the men in the village have no minds when they are very old and they just walk about all crazy and not knowing about things.

He gave up looking for the mosquitoes that were

there somewhere and would find him later tonight, unless he got under the mosquito net the right way, and, setting the lantern on the table and picking up a book, sat down to read.

I hope I can finish the book by this weekend, he thought in the chair in the light of the lantern, then it will have been four this month. That's one a week, and that's pretty good. I'll try and read more, and then after Christmas, two a week, unless they are big ones. And if the ones on Africa come I can read all of them and get to know things good about this place. Then I can read even more and get to where I'm reading a lot of good books a lot of the time and then I can just read a lot. I hope that I can get some good ones, though, and start learning again. I haven't been learning that much. I could read about something, and learn about it, and then get good at it. This is a good place to read while living here in this place with nothing to do but wait around in the forest and try not to daydream.

Outside in the darkness, the crickets sounded like heavy traffic in a city: a loud, high roar. And in the distance, voices from the village could sometimes be heard laughing or talking, but they were only faint sounds coming through the roar of the crickets that were everywhere in the fields surrounding the house. At times you could hear individual crickets that made strange cricket sounds or that were louder than the rest, but mostly it was a screeching roar.

Sitting in the soft chair in the lantern-lit room,

wrapped in the towel, the man opened the book and began to read, while, outside in the warm night air, the crickets told each other about what they had learned.

*   *   *

He awoke suddenly in the darkness of the room on his bed under the mosquito net, and, in his mind, soaring high into the night air above the house, saw below the thick forest surrounding the house and covering the low hills around the village, and, soaring higher into the dark night air, far below in all directions hills and thick forest, and, scattered about near the small winding streams and on the dark valley floors, small villages and towns speckled with the faint glow of lantern light. And then nothing but forest: dark, still, too still down around the ground where it was darkest; and now laterally through the air forty miles to the west and a town shimmering below with the bright glow of electric lights. Then rapidly to the south, following high above a dark ribbon of road winding through the forest, the forest draping over the road, the road coming back out again; faster through the dark night air and now another glowing village and the forest suddenly giving way to the drier coastal belt and the dark road straight and clear and then the road ending and a sudden white stripe of surf-pounded beach and now high out over the dark Atlantic, the swell-covered surface shimmering below in the moon-lit night. Then, back again above the house to the north: forest covered hills and small winding roads in the darkness below. Now northward from the house and tiny villages of speckled lantern light again, sprinkled about in all directions on the dark forest floor; on a hundred miles and a hundred miles more and the forest giving slowly way to the dry northern savanna; faster still through the dark night air and now towering escarpments of the Sahel, stretching out below to each side into the distance, passing under quickly, and then sand coming into the valleys between the escarpments and then mostly sand and the Sahara stretching to the north for a thousand miles.

Awake now on the bed, his eyes widened as, through the cracks around the wood shutters of the windows, the bright light of the moon-lit night seeped into the dark room.

Oh, god, he thought, there in the room with the roar of the crickets outside deafening, it is the night and I was there again, there with those ones again. Damn it to damn: you cannot get away, you cannot get them out of you; you can go far away, leave and go a long ways away, to the other side of the world, to the dark forests of *Ashanti* where the gold and slaves flowed thick for three hundred years; go there and live in a small house that is surrounded by deep forest and the people still carry the old charms to keep the juju away; but the ones who had been bad to you and made you cry hard when you were young will come in the night and give you no choice about where you are and take you away and hurt you again. And the night will put you in places that you don't know how you got to, and with people who you don't know what you are doing with; all still there in you and alive and laughing and more alive than before, and liking to see you more than before, and very glad to have you around and glad that we could all be together again and saying: wait, now, you aren't going anywhere; and go ahead and try, and let's spend some time together, good time, fun time, very fun time: *and here have this*; all very deep in you and coming out late in the night and then you awake in the dark and have to remember that you are here in this place with the crickets. And you think, clearly, where it is you are, and you are alone and know that the morning won't come for a very long time; not until the night is through with you and is tired of you because it is the night and it does what it wants with you. It doesn't have anything better to do so it does things with you: sends you places and has you be with certain people; and it may be people with whom you would rather not be but you don't have any choice because you have to go where the night takes you. And when you awake you feel the scare: bad; and deep; and then the morning comes and the night goes away because it does not like the light, and when you get up the scare goes too.

He lay awake in the darkness on the bed under

the mosquito net, and, calmer, knew now where he was; and he was soon asleep again as the crickets continued outside, but not as loudly.

In the morning he awoke and was tired and could hear the people out on the road going to farm. The air was cool and he felt comfortable lying on his back on the soft mattress. He pulled the mosquito net back and got up and went over and opened the wood shutters to let in the bright morning light. The green valley floor spread out beyond the road and he could see the straight rows of the palm oil trees in the distance, and, beyond, the forest-covered hills, all in the pleasant morning light.

The man dressed and went into the kitchen and lit the kerosene cooker to make breakfast. He boiled water for coffee and sliced the small piece of bread that had come with the evening's dinner to eat with the creamy paste of groundnuts. There were no more tins of milk so he would have to drink the coffee black. Sitting at the plywood table, he ate the bread and drank the coffee while listening to the calls of the people to each other on the road on their way to farm in the cool morning air.

Tomorrow I will go down to Tom's in Takoradi on the coast to see Tom and Mitch and Laurie, who will be coming in from Assini, he thought at the table in the sun-lit kitchen. I'm going to go down there after all, instead of staying around here for the weekend and tutoring the students. At Tom's, with the large house and the range and refrigerator, and the full bathroom, and being in a large city with electric lights, it is like going to stay at a big hotel. And Mitch and Laurie will be there and no one has seen Laurie since July. She's been by herself in Assini since July and said that she finally had to leave it for a while and would go to Tom's. And Mitch will come over from Sekondi and he will have all the magazines for October and maybe a *Herald Tribune*; and Tom was in Accra two weeks ago and so he should have all the mail that went there. And there is more food in Takoradi than anyplace else in the Western Region and we can all go out to a club and get beer easy; and there will be many people around, and, down there in the big cities on the coast, they are more used to the Europeans and so will not call out to us so much. But it won't matter even if they do laugh, or call out, or if the children follow us around, because it will be the four of us again and the four of us have not been together since last Christmas, ten months ago, and we won't care about anything and can talk a lot and find out about what has been going on. And there is a lot to find out. Like with Bob; what has been going on with Bob? I haven't heard anything since the letter Mitch sent a month ago and he had been to the Eastern Region to see Bob and had said that Bob was talking about going home. He said Bob was feeling bad, and had been sick most of the last dry season, and did not like it anymore. The teaching part was going bad, too, and he did not think that he could stay much longer. ...I hope he doesn't go. I hope he stays and doesn't go back to Michigan, or Ohio, wherever it is he's from. He should just stay and go with us to the white-sand beach at Busua at the Easter time, or at least up to the game reserve again. But that is such a hard trip to make to the game reserve; it is very hard from the Tamale to Damango part. You can get to Tamale, okay, but then you have to wait for two days for a truck that is going out to Damamgo and it is very hot standing by the road and if you can't get a ride early then you can't get back to town in time to find a place to stay for the night and standing out on the road the heat takes everything out of you. And even if you do get a ride to Damango, even a good one: in a government Peugeot that is going out and they go fast on the dirt parts and make it in two hours and stop for you at the *Nzima* villages along the way so you can take pictures of the painted compound walls; and the government people give you food or beer in exchange for your address in America so that they may correspond with you later; even then you can be stuck in Damango for the night and have to walk into the game reserve the next morning and in April during the dry season that is a very hard thing to do because the sun will take all the water out of your skin in three hours. But I hope Bob stays, and, anyway, we can all go to the ocean and swim in the surf and buy beer at the hotel; even if they make us pay eight cedis a bottle. The bastards. But he should just stay here. If he can just last at his school for six more months then he can go to the coast with us and get feeling good again; unless they don't have much food there and we have to eat the bad coast kenkey. But I just hope they'll have more food around this place so that we can get better food to eat. Jesus-the-Christer it is tough to get the foods. Now, there's no food around this place, but, this is something, if you get in a bus at Tarkwa Station and can put up with the bad roads to the west for two days, you come to a border in the jungle and ten feet over the border is all the food in the world. I'm not kidding. Right now, from here, you go one hundred miles to the west through the thick forest and low mountains and when you get to the border at the end of the day all they have there is food. All good food and you can eat it all day long and then fill up your pack to bring some back; but even if you bring back a lot you'll eat it all in one week and then what are you going to do? Hmmm? You can't make that trip every week; it would kill you up bad. But the food they have there is all good; good food. And it is all there and you can go right there and buy it and eat it, and it is good eating it. And now I will tell you what the thing is about this food—no, maybe I should not tell. Maybe it would be best that I did not tell you what the very special thing is about this most glorious food. But, all right, I do not want you to become angry and so I will tell. ...No—maybe I sh... No...all right. I will. Now listen: and to dammit I am telling the truth. Now, listen: it is all from the country of France. *Really!* You go through the hot African jungle on a bus that should not be on any road and is packed full with too many people and breaks down four times on the way; and you are riding through the thick western rain forest and it takes eighteen hours and there is only the coast kenkey to eat, up four days from the coast that the young girls sell through the bus windows in the villages along the way, and then the bus breaks out of the forest and crosses a bridge over a wide river and there is the border and then nothing but rows and rows of shacks, all very full with the good food of the France country. France is four-thousand miles away but you are eating the good food of France just one hundred miles from here; and buying it. Maybe I wouldn't have come to this place if I had known about the food. How can you be in a place where you can't do anything because you have to think about foods? There will be some, anyway, at Tom's. And Laurie will be there to tell about the road to Assini and if it is better than to go up through Sunyani. How is Laurie? I wonder how she is. She has been out there a long time. That place is a long ways out, further out than any of the schools down here in the south, almost as far as the places in the north. I can't wait to go up north at Christmas. I should go up there. But how does Laurie stay in Assini? Her school isn't that good, I don't think. It's got the good houses for the teachers to stay in, but the Nationals who are out there don't want to be at it. How can she stay? How can I? I've got to go down to Tom's for sure. I've got to go down there this weekend and not try and stay around and just do the work in the school. You can become troubled here... But you shouldn't try and stay around too much. You should get out and try and stay away from the bad places; but I'm telling you it's not so bad all the time. I can get food from the school, and they'll give me a lot. Laurie must get foods from her school. She must be getting the food from there. But maybe she gets money sent from home and has someone going to the border to bring back good food. She could hire someone to go there and bring it back. I don't know. No one has heard from her in two months. I haven't seen her either. Maybe the magazines will be at Tom's and I can bring them back and find out about everything. I hope I can get the bus easy to go there. It should be easy to do.

He got up from the table in the kitchen and poured the half cup of now cold coffee into the sink and then set the cup in the plastic wash bowl, and, going into his room and collecting his books for the day's teaching, went out to the road and down to the school.

*   *   *

In the late afternoon of the following day, the man walked into the village with his light travel-pack and caught the last Datsun run going to the busy mining town of Tarkwa, twenty miles to the west, where, upon arriving, he boarded the night bus for the coast. He did not see the British engineer, whom he had never seen, whom he was told lived alone in a house somewhere near the mine. He only knew about the man because the people of Tarkwa, whenever he came there, would tell him they had *seen his brother that day*, near the market, or at the post office, or in the government food store.

The crowded bus left Tarkwa in the heat of the early evening and turned onto the rough, potholed highway at the edge of town and roared down the highway for the coast, the green hues of the forest-covered hills in the distance darkening with the setting sun, the thick jungle and undergrowth pushing in on both sides of the narrow road, the streams and rivers still swollen from the late-afternoon rains; on into the heavy bamboo groves of the lowlands, the thick shoots soaring like fireworks into the air and then leaning over the road to form a dark, solid canopy under which the bus passed; on through the palm oil and rubber tree plantations of the south, mile after mile of perfect rows stretching away from each side into the horizon; then the forest giving way to the drier coastal belt of coconut palms and high grasses; and now the food stalls and the people and the lighted outskirts of Takoradi.

Carrying his travel pack on his back in the humid coastal heat, he moved quickly from the bus station through the thick night crowds of the city, out to the southernmost edge where an old school compound rested quietly on the hillside overlooking the ocean. In the distance were the lights of the ships in the harbor, and, listening carefully in the still, evening air, he could hear the low roar of surf crashing on the beach below. Entering through the main gate of the dark, hillside compound, he walked quickly down the steeply sloping pavement to the front steps of a large, single-story cement house near the center of the compound, and, climbing the steps to the front porch, stopped and set down his pack. Now he stood in the darkness of the porch and looked at the soft glow of the electric lights coming through the heavily screened windows of the house. There had been electric lights in the city, too, and vehicles with bright headlights driving about, but moving rapidly so as not to draw the crowd's attention, he had noticed them only fleetingly. Now on the porch he let himself be bathed by their glow. From within the house he could also hear the dull whine of the overhead ceiling fan, and, although he could not make out the words, and coming with a kind of metallic-resonance because of the fan, the rapid-fire bursts of people talking. He remained at the top of the steps in the glow of the lights. He had been at the village to the north for over two months this time, and he knew that a change came over him whenever he went to it. Standing quietly in the dark compound, he knew that he was still in the change, and that it made him different; and he knew that he could make it go away by reaching out and knocking on the wood porch door and he thought that he didn't want it to go away and that he liked the change and he played with it not going away by remaining on the top of the dark steps in the humid evening air with the buzzing of the insects in the grasses between the houses and the roar of the surf on the beach below. Then from somewhere came the thought of how frightening it would be if maybe there was something under the dark trees between the houses at his back, and, standing at the top of the steps in the soft glow of the lights, a cold chill came slowly up his spine and he tried not to think about there maybe being something there and to think about other things; anything; going up north: Jim and I will go up north; and he thought of the arid north with the sun-scorched hills. But he quickly came back to the dark area under the trees; and, no: I'll go to the north; but the chill grew, and, standing on the porch with his back to the trees, he slowly turned and strained to see under them, and then quickly looked away. But his eyes came back to the dark area between the houses and he felt the pounding of his heart and strained again to see under the trees and then the change that had followed him from his village to the north left and went off into the dark night sky and whatever was under the trees went off with it and he turned and knocked hard on the wood porch door.

TWO

The pitch of the voices in the house rose, the door swung open, and the bright electric lights spilled out onto the porch, blinding the traveler. Silhouetted in the doorway was the tall, thin figure of a man.

"Roger!" It was Tom, who lived in the house. "You made it down."

The traveler, standing beside his pack on the porch, looked at the thinness of the house owner's frame, and the strange-looking, paisley-patterned shirt and loose-fitting corduroy pants he was wearing.

"Are you alive?" asked the house owner.

"I'm alive," said the traveler.

His face was spotted with dirt and sweat, and, reaching down and picking up his pack, he stepped into the brightly-lit house.

"We didn't know if you were coming down for sure," said the house owner. "—*Laurie!*" he called back into the house. "Look who's here."

A woman came into the entryway. She saw the traveler and stopped.

"Roger!—is it you?"

"I made it all the way down."

"What's been going on up there?"

"I don't know. Everything. I left after school and got to Tarkwa Station. They were selling rice and lamb for three cedis. I got a good bus and just got here. Where's Mitch?"

"He should be over," said the house owner. "Come in—sit down."

They went into the main room of the house where a narrow couch and several cushioned chairs were arranged in a half circle around a low, wood table. The traveler and the woman sat down on the couch as the house owner went into the kitchen. He quickly returned with a large wine bottle, filled with cold water that he stored in the refrigerator, and three glasses. He poured the water into the glasses and sat in one of the chairs. They raised their glasses into the air, took several small sips, and prepared to talk. Overhead, the ceiling fan whined loudly.

"Mitch said he'd come over when I talked to him last week and he heard that people were going to be coming," said the house owner. "He said he saw Bob last month."

"Good," said the traveler. "I have to find out what Bob is going to do."

"You got rice and lamb for three cedis?" asked the woman. "It was four in Assini all week, and with just a little piece of meat."

"They were selling it," said the traveler. "But, Laurie, where have you been?"

"I had to come out of that place, Roger; I had to get out. But do you know how hard it is getting in and out of there? I had to take a truck that left at four in the morning so I had to get up at three to get a seat in the cab, so I wouldn't die on the way here. And then we didn't get here until after five this afternoon. But no breakdowns—the whole way. I haven't been out of Assini for three months."

"But what do you have to do there?"

"All I do is teach all day and then try to help those poor market women organize their co-op."

"We hadn't heard what was going on," said the traveler. "Can you get food?"

"No. The school can't get any either."

"Can you get enough of it though?"

"No. It never makes it out there."

"I know," said the traveler. "It's hard to get even in Tarkwa. The office should just send it out from Accra. Tom, can you get bread?"

"We can get it at the UST store in the morning. I know the owner. I can get it."

"But, really, when is Mitch coming over?"

"I know, he should be over," said the house owner.

"Will he bring the magazines?"

"I told him to be sure to bring them."

"I haven't gotten any in over a month," said the traveler. "So I don't know anything."

"Someone tried to shoot the president," said the woman.

"No."

"They got the guy."

"No—what, was he crazy?"

"I don't know. I haven't read about it."

"I don't want to go back there," said the traveler. "Ever."

"Don't go back," said the woman. "We can all stay here and become farmers."

"Except there wouldn't be any trees left after Roger drank all the palm wine," said the house owner.

"*Ha!*" said the woman. "You're right. And it would just speed up the advancing desert."

"No, now, I can't drink that stuff anymore," said the traveler. "But, Laurie, really, are you going to make it in Assini? I wrote last month but I don't know if it made it."

"Nothing came; but I don't know what's been going on. I was sick for two weeks and couldn't eat. And we've had to eat rice with the bad river fish for the last month at the school because the headmaster takes all the tins of mackerel to his house for his family. He doesn't like it out there, so he keeps all the food for himself. None of the other masters like him."

"Really? What about the ocean?"

"There's one good beach that I can go to," said the woman. "You know, I've got to have the ocean. I couldn't make it here without the sea—except most of the beach is too steep."

"I know," said the house owner. "But I think we should all go to the beach at Busua tomorrow."

"I'm willing to go out there with you," said the woman.

"I really want to go—bad," said the traveler.

"We'll just leave here early tomorrow and go," said the house owner.

"Good," said the woman.

"You know, Laurie, I'm supposed to be going up north at Christmas, don't you?" said the traveler.

"With Jim, right?"

"He said he wanted to go up there. I can't wait. Ron might go, too. And I heard from Lloyd that Karen is going up there with Scott, but they're going to leave before Christmas, so I don't know if we'll see them or not. You know, though, she isn't going to be going up with Peter. She won't go with him. I don't think she'll even be around him anymore. But maybe she'll decide to."

"How do you know?" the woman asked.

"I don't, it's what Scott said."

"Really?" said the house owner.

"How was Lloyd doing?" the woman asked. "I haven't seen him since we were in Accra together last March, and we ended up drinking way too much beer on the last night. We had at least three bottles of *Club*, each, at Chez´ Marie Lou, and that disco that's across the street."

"They had beer?" asked the house owner.

"A lot," said the woman. "And they were selling it at control price."

"Really?"

"But you should have seen Lloyd," said the woman. "He kept trying to make it with all these Nigerian girls, but none of them would go with him. And then the next morning I had to take the coast train back, and Lloyd said he was taking the bus to Tema to try and buy science supplies for his school."

"Lloyd was?" asked the traveler.

"He was supposed to."

"Did any of you hear that Sharon went back?" asked the house owner.

"No," said the woman, looking up.

"For good?" asked the traveler.

"She terminated. She finally went back for good, in September."

"No. You're kidding," said the woman.

"She gave up, Laurie. She didn't like it at her school. And Karen said she kept running out of money."

"No. I still don't believe it," said the woman. "*Sharon!* How could you? We had so much fun together during training, you know? And she didn't even write to tell me!"

"I was surprised, too," said the house owner. "And you heard about Doug and Peter getting robbed on the beach in Accra, didn't you?"

"I heard," said the woman. "You can't go around that part anymore, even during the day."

"It isn't any good for swimming there, anyway," said the traveler.

"I don't know," said the woman.

"Roger, take a look at this book," said the house owner. "You've got to read it."

"Is it any good?"

"It's a pretty good book, but, here, take it."

The house owner handed the traveler a thick, beat-up paperback with a dark blue cover that had been sitting on the end of the table.

"Do you need it back?"

"No. Mitch gave it to me, so you can pass it on."

"I hope he hurries and gets over here."

"Do you have to get back?" asked the woman.

"I have classes Monday morning, so I'll take the late bus on Sunday. How long are you going to stay?"

"I'm taking the train to Accra Monday morning. I have to check on some money that was supposed to come. And the medical staff wants me to come in for more shots. Do you need anything from Accra?"

"Yes, definitely. Bring some tins of milk and a tin of margarine, if you can get any. Tom can pay you when you get back, and then I can pay him when I come down again."

"I'll be going into the Accra market. I should at least be able to find some margarine."

"Good. I need some bad."

"I should be back here by Wednesday."

"Good. I can come back down in a few weeks, it's pretty easy getting down here."

"I want to know about Sheila, though," said the house owner. "Did she really end up marrying that National who was out at her school? Do you know?"

"Sheila?" asked the traveler. "Oh, now, wait—she was kind of skinny, right? And she was stationed at—where—Kejebi, right?"

"Right. They had her out there," said the woman. "And she was supposed to marry the National. You remember, she was the one always running around with Peter and Karen and all those people during training. Don't you?"

"No, I barely remember," said the traveler. "But wasn't she the one always giving her eggs out at breakfast during training, because she couldn't eat them? People were going crazy for eggs, and she'd give hers away."

"But what about Kenny?" asked the house owner. "He had the worst time with the food. He must have lost twenty-five pounds in what, four weeks, because he couldn't eat the stews they kept serving? And then he just ended up buying chocolate bars and taking them up to the library to eat every night."

"You know, though," said the traveler, "I saw Kenny at the airport with all those people who were going back on that flight last July; it was when Colleen was going back, and there were all those people on that same flight: Liz was going back, and Doug and June, and those two kind of strange guys who had dinner with us at the Jade Garden around Easter, remember them?"

"No, not really."

"They were stationed out at the small school along the coast on the way to Lome´."

"I kind of remember them," said the woman.

"But, so; when I saw Kenny at the airport, he said he was planning on staying a third year. Can you believe that?"

"I guess I can," said the house owner.

"How long did he go back for?" asked the woman.

"Two months. I heard two full months. He must have had a good time."

"And that was when Liz went back, though?" asked the house owner.

"Right. She went back then," said the traveler. "She made up her mind to go, but I don't know why. Really, there's no way she should have gone; it's because of her house. And did you see her school?"

"I never did," said the woman.

"You couldn't help but like her school. I saw it and her house last Christmas, back when Downey was still there, and they had everything at that place, those two had everything. You could just go over and turn on the ceiling fan if you wanted to and the house would cool right down. And the refrigerator was standard size. Shit, I mean, it must have been hauled into there on the Kumasi line. I'm not kidding either. The place was even better than here."

"I'm pretty lucky to have this place," said the house owner. "There's almost always electricity, and the beach is pretty good out a ways."

"But even with a place like Liz had, it's still hard to stay," said the traveler. "I don't know."

"I know," said the woman. "But think about it, what would you do back in the States, besides eat?"

"I know."

"You'd eat for three weeks, and go to all the movies you've missed, and maybe a few baseball games. But then you'd have to go out and get a job. Can you imagine that? Can you imagine going out and working at a job, what, forty hours a week?"

"I couldn't do it," said the house owner.

"I know I couldn't," said the woman. "I can't."

"No," said the traveler. "Not after here."

"I know."

"And besides," said the traveler, "what kind of job would you try and get?"

"I know. You should just go home and try and write your memoirs," said the house owner.

"That's what I thought I was going to do here," said the traveler, "but I didn't know what it was going to be like."

"You can't," said the house owner.

"If anyone did, no one would ever come," said the woman. "Look at Malcom, he lasted, what, three days? And people have died. And remember the bus ride from the airport?"

"Yes, god," said the house owner.

"You have to be lucky not to get medivaced, or lose your school, or just leave," said the woman. "Did you know that Cindy left her school in Accra?"

"She got a new school?" asked the traveler.

"She's supposed to be trying to get into the Volta Region is what I heard," said the house owner. "She might try and take Mike's place, but the office doesn't know if they should send someone out there yet, after Mike just left in the middle of the term. They're going to let her leave her school, though. She couldn't stay there any longer with Patti."

"I don't blame her," said the traveler. "I really don't blame her at all. I don't know how she lasted a whole year there with Patti. I wouldn't have lasted that long."

"I know what you mean," said the woman.

"Remember having to listen to her in training during language lessons?" asked the traveler.

"I know."

"She just couldn't stop talking. She'd spend twenty minutes everyday telling everyone about all the medical schools she was going to apply to, because she had to be a doctor. And then Ossei would have to keep us there for another ten minutes into lunch so we wouldn't get too far behind, and then we'd get stuck eating all the fish-heads."

"I still can't eat them," said the house owner.

"I can eat them every now and then," said the traveler.

"But, right, there was something about Patti," the house owner said. "Do you remember the time during training when she started talking about Barbara Walters, and how she thought Barbara Walters was the ideal woman? And she wasn't kidding either."

"Maybe she's her daughter," said the woman.

"No, right, she'll probably name one of her children 'Barbara'," said the traveler. He laughed.

"I just hope Cindy gets a new school," said the woman.

"She should," said the house owner, "they need teachers even worse this year."

"But it's hard living with another American out at a school if you don't get along with them," said the woman.

"Darrel about drove me out of my mind during training," said the traveler. "And there were, what, eighty of us then? Him and the guy that got sent to Koforidua. I'm lucky he moved away."

"I don't know; how do people like that end up coming here?" asked the woman.

"But if you think they were strange," said the traveler, "wait until you meet the new agricultural-extension people. The ones who came last May. Do you know who I mean?"

"No."

"They're out of their minds. Really. They're not normal. All they do is go into Accra every weekend and get drunk like you can't believe. They drink there all the time. And last September I was staying at the Presby and they were there having a meeting or something with the office, and everyday, by three, at the very latest, they'd be over at Jauques drinking *Red Knight*, or down at that bar by the main post office, getting drunk there. And then later they'd go to one of the good restaurants on Cantoments, or out by the airport, and be drinking more. And they'd be yelling and arguing and the people wouldn't know what to do."

"Are you kidding?" said the woman.

"No, I'm not. One night we went to the Tropicana with a few of them and this one guy almost got in a fight with the head-waiter over the bill."

"You're kidding."

"No. They're all pretty young, though; like twenty, twenty-one. I've seen them in Accra a few times and at the Presby and they're always drunk."

"Who did you say they are?" asked the house owner.

"They're new agricultural people. They came in May."

"And they're all at sites around Accra?" asked the woman.

"I'm pretty sure," said the traveler. "I think they're all in the Central Region. Except for one guy in the Volta. There's a good chance that you'll run into them in Accra, Laurie."

"I'll probably see them somewhere."

"You can't miss them."

"Hey," said the house owner, "is anyone getting hungry?"

"I wouldn't mind something before long," said the traveler.

"Good. We should start thinking about something for tonight. We can go over to Amoah's flat, or we can bring back some beans, and I've got rice and fish to cook."

"Did you tell Amoah we were going to be here?" asked the traveler.

"I told him some friends were coming in."

"Let's just get something to bring back and we can go to Amoah's tomorrow when Mitch is here," said the traveler.

"After we go out to Busua," said the woman.

"Right, clear out to the lagoon," said the traveler. "So let's go find some beans to bring back. Are you ready to go, Laurie?"

"I just need my bag."

Moving to the edge of the couch, the woman stood up.

"Go toward the market," said the house owner. "You'll see some plantain stands, and there'll be rice and beans around. I'll start getting the fish ready."

"We shouldn't be too long," said the traveler.

The man who had come from the village stood up from the couch.

"Good, I'll start getting things ready," said the house owner.

"Okay, let's go," said the woman.

The traveler and the woman went out the door, and, leaving the bright lights of the bungalow, headed in darkness toward the center of town to look for the hot cooked beans that were sold at lantern-lit tables lining the streets around the central market. And later that evening, after a large, hot meal at Tom's, Mitch came in from his neighboring school with two months of magazines, half of which he gave to Roger and the other half to Laurie, and then later still, after cushions from the couches were spread onto the living room floor, stayed the night, where Roger also slept; and the two talked long into the night as overhead the ceiling fan continued to spin. And the next day they all went by crowded bus ten miles up the humid coast to the white-sand beach at Busua and swam in the warm ocean and ate pounded yam with hot soup at the dirt-floor food bar in the fishing village at the far end of the beach. And then that night back at Tom's, another large meal, over at Mr. Amoah's flat, the school's science teacher, cooked specially for the out-of-town visitors by his wife, Eunice. And then late on Sunday, Tom, Laurie, and Mitch walked with Roger back to the central market to look for some food items for Roger to take back to his school, and, finding some tins of corned-beef and a small bag of coffee, walked with him to the dusty open-air bus station to see him off to Tarkwa and his village beyond. Standing in the hot afternoon sun at the crowded station, they said their good byes.

"It looks like a good bus, Roger" said the house owner, looking over the brightly-painted, Tarkwa-bound vehicle. "The ride shouldn't be too bad."

"It should be able to make it pretty fast at this time of day," said the traveler.

"When will you be back down?"

"I'll try and come down in a few weeks. Laurie should be able to find some food stuffs in Accra somewhere."

"I'll look everyplace I can think of," said the woman.

"So, Mitch, are you going to make it up this term?"

The traveler looked at the short, stocky, red-faced man from the nearby coastal school standing beside him.

"I'm really going to try to get away, Roger. I really want to see that part of the Western Region, and the rain forest. Can we go out into the forest at all?"

"There are some trails right around my house. There's a ridge we can go up."

"Good, I'll try and come up."

"All right. Good," said the traveler. "Now, everyone get out of this sun; it's too hot out here. And I'll see you at Christmas. You're coming in for Christmas aren't you, Laurie?"

"I'm working on the party, so I'll definitely be coming."

"Good. Then get out of this sun. Good bye. And take care."

"Good bye, Roger," the three people each said to the traveler.

The man climbed into the crowded bus as the others left to go back to Tom's, and soon the bus was weaving it's way through the maze of dirt streets out to the edge of the city where it turned onto the highway and sped toward Tarkwa, four hours to the north. Out the open window the man watched the endless stream of lightly-dressed people with large produce baskets on their head's walking along the side of the narrow road on their way from the farms back to their villages, and, as the bus approached, each carefully stepping into the tall grasses bordering the road and then watching as the bus roared by.

At the outskirts of an approaching village, where the dirt shoulder grew wide, two small-boys were jumping up and down and waving at the steady stream of passing vehicles; and as the bus approached the man turned his head and looked straight out the open window at them and the two small-boys, startled, leaped back on the dirt strip when they saw his face in the crowded bus, and then with widened eyes chased excitedly after the bus as it quickly sped away.

Looking again out the front windscreen, the man watched the forest covered inland-hills approaching in the distance. I hope the boy is around to bring tonight's meal from the school, he thought, watching the forest. Damn it, if he's not, I'll have to go and get it myself.

With the Fish and the Flies

The green and yellow Honda taxi stopped quickly in a cloud of dust and the two American passengers paid the two-hundred CFA fare to the driver and got out into the mid-afternoon sun; there at the border on the coast of West Africa and it was hot even with the breeze blowing in off the ocean as the surf pounded the beach a hundred yards away. The beer the young man Mitchell Gray had drank just before they had gotten into the taxi now felt good, and it felt familiar, and with the girl there he felt even better. This would be the difficult part, though: crossing the border and then finding a car to take them the hundred and forty miles on to Accra. But they were ready for it now: they had drank beer all afternoon; there at the outdoor bar across the street from the crowded central market, only a small section of the market visible to them, but that section extending in each direction for as far as they could see; next to the taxi station, the rush of taxis on the dirt street stirring up the dust; and everywhere the mass of traders hawking their goods, everywhere the mass of people; and the blue Atlantic pounding the beach a hundred yards away and the beer had been devilishly good and they had held arms, not hands, but arms, and talked meaningfully.

Crossing the borders and riding in the crowded buses and cars was the most difficult part and the beer could only do so much, but it was the best way to go about it; definitely. Mitchell led them through the crowd carrying his large soft pack on his back, and the blond-haired girl with her frame pack and shoulder bag followed closely behind. She could see it was best that Mitchell led, and she didn't mind, and Mitchell knew he would make it much easier for her by leading, he knew this was something he had learned to do well in Africa: and doing it well he led them to the first line and on to where the inspector was, still outside, and told the man without words that he and the girl were not any trouble, that they were hot and uncomfortable and just wanted to get through as quickly as possible. And the tall African border man who spoke only French and his tribal language anyway, and wouldn't have understood Mitchell's English anyway, told Mitchell back without words that he understood, as he smiled broadly at people above and beyond Mitchell's shoulder, and stamped Mitchell and the blond-haired girl, Liz's, passports and then looked only briefly into their bags.

Now they were in the middle of the crossing. Shouts and pointing hands guided them on to the next station, pushed them on ahead of a mass of perspiring black faces that made up a line that seemed never to move no matter how hard or fast the inspectors at the tables were working; on to where the officials now spoke English, and asked the young American couple who were still feeling pleasant from the beer, who were now without thoughts, only the pure emotion of the boiling kettle they were in, what fine goods they were bringing in, and when hearing Mitchell tell them what they had, let them go on, without checking Mitchell's words, to the last office, now inside, where everyone wore dark glasses and smiled often; and there a final inspection and stamping of Mitchell and Liz's visa's and then out the door and they were now over the border and it was suddenly calmer.

"That wasn't too bad," Mitchell said.

"It could have been much worse," she said.

"We didn't have much but they might have taken some of it anyway, and then we wouldn't have had hardly anything."

"They might have taken some of my soap," she said. "There are only five bars but I really need them. I haven't had any good soap for so long."

Mitchell thought how he hadn't been with a good

girl for so long, and this one was good. It had developed the way he liked best, unexpectedly and without a sense of desperation or fear of loss if it stopped working out. But even though he knew this girl was special, he did not praise her like he had thought he would if he had ever managed somehow to have a special one interested in him, as she seemed to be. Then, there in the heat just over the border, a thought without words, having traveled a great distance, stopped to rest near Mitchell and then quickly left as he continued to lead them along; there on the dirt road lined with the cars that sometimes made it to their destinations, the thrown together wood kiosks behind the cars, and the dust and the people and there, dominating to the south, the Atlantic; it was peaceful out there, and Mitchell turned suddenly and pulled her to him.

He thought back to the night before on the beach after the eating and drinking in the bars in town, the good bars, not expensive but good, mostly local, some filled with the French but most with the damn coastal *Fanti* and *Ewé* who had money, and the food was good, better than what they had been eating at the schools; and Mitchell had made a pass at the girl there on the beach, in a way that he knew would be good even if she turned away. But she hadn't turned away from the pass that Mitchell Gray had dreamed up from somewhere far away only moments before, and had made her laugh, and made them both feel that this was as good as it could be: two young Americans on a beach in the night in Africa.

"Where's our car, Mitch? Where's that twenty-cedi Benz you said would be waiting?" She was laughing in the heat and dust there at the border. And she tugged on his arm and pulled him down and kissed his lip and jaw; and Mitch tried to suppress a smile. Something was causing her to do this he thought as he led them on, there amongst the traders, the children without shoes coming up close, the women in the shade pointing and laughing, the men calling out; so he would continue doing whatever it was he had been doing, being however it was he was being; there in the dust and the crowd, leading them on until they found a car, a good one, even if they had to pay extra, what the hell.

"What the hell," he said.

She did not answer. She was looking out toward the ocean, out through the tall palms just up from the sand bending back toward the land. She was out there now, her face to the breeze gently blowing her hair, and now coming back, turning and looking up at Mitchell, and seeing he was looking at her, looking quickly away, and then reaching for his arm.

"Let's go over there and make out," he said. "This boy here will watch our bags and then we can go over there behind those kiosks."

And he was saying this as though he were not serious, which he knew it must not sound, for why in God's name would two Americans without a car, in need of transport, there in the rapidly approaching evening at the border on the coast of Africa, amongst the maddening mass of people, without room or food, in the dust and heat and with a long and crowded ride ahead, if they could find one, the salt smell of the ocean mixing with the racks of fish drying in the sun and covered with flies, the crying children, the crowd calling out to them constantly, never letting them forget they were seen, in a land so far away, why would they ever stand behind some wood shacks, a crowd back there, and make out, in the heat?

And he asked her again.

And now he could see it was she who suppressing a smile. Who was this person who would have such a thought, she must be thinking. Who would have thought that thought here in this place? But in his heart he knew it was serious, not the actual going somewhere and kissing, or not going somewhere and not kissing, but that it was something that must be brought into the world, this thought, from wherever it is before it is brought out and made to exist, made a part of it all.

And without going behind a kiosk to make out, there in the ending afternoon in the crowd, they walked on with the weight of their packs pulling down hard onto their backs as the sweat under their shirts soaked through to the packs and the dust did not cake where they were still dry.

Soon, he thought, they would be in a car riding

through the flatlands back to Accra. And in Accra, he back to his room in the rest house and she back to the room at the American Consulate's home. And the next day, after a final rush for more supplies in Accra, on, separately, to their schools in the mountains and back to the fear that called in the night. The fear that called with a pounding from the isolation in the mountains that ate at you slowly in the daylight when the crowds surrounded you always, and later alone in your room in the night when you awoke suddenly in the darkness, and could make out nothing for sure on the walls, and listening into the distance could hear nothing for sure, but there in your room, clearly, something, and then realizing it was coming from within, listened frighteningly to that which you knew now to be the pounding of your heart.

At the border, paying the Peugeot driver fifty cedis and climbing into the back, their hands came apart and they did not touch again.

Death in the Morning

The old men came slowly up the dirt road that led to the school from the village and when the children in the classes first saw them they began to murmur excitedly. The Headmaster and the school messenger came out onto the veranda to greet them, and the iron hand bell was rung cutting off early the second class of the hot African morning. The students, still talking excitedly, gathered in clusters around their classrooms as the teachers came out to where the Chief and the Elders were now in a loud but friendly discussion with the Headmaster and the messenger and the man who had the goat on a rope; and the goat jerked and bleated loudly because it had never been tied to the end of a rope before.

There had been much illness amongst the students lately, more so than anyone could recall since the school had opened three years before, and this rash of illnesses had come to the attention of the Elders and it was decided that a goat would be killed, as was customary in such situations.

The Chief and the Elders and the officials from the school walked across the field to where the small stream cut through the edge of the school grounds, and the man with the goat tied it tightly and closely to a hard branch on the bank. There was less than six inches from the branch to the goat's neck and the goat, its neck red and bleeding from the rope, its bleating faint and distant, waited for the certainty in the men around it to end.

The Old Man Who Forgot His Shoes

He was an old man and he was riding on the crowded bus between Cape Coast and Takoradi and at a small village along the road, just before Takoradi, the bus pulled on over. The old man got up from his seat near the back and made his way through the many people and got down off the bus. On the dirt, he began walking slowly toward the village when suddenly he turned quickly around and began calling excitedly back toward the bus in his native tongue; and what he was saying caused the people on the bus to begin laughing, some of them quite loudly. The old man hurried back onto the bus and made his way again through the many people as they continued to laugh at what he had said. He made it back to the seat where he had been sitting and there he reached down to floor and picked up an old pair of shoes. The old man had forgotten his shoes and this is why the people were laughing. It may have been that he was not use to them.

Motion

There is a small flat grassy spot next to the dirt-track road and everywhere close in, except for the road and this grassy spot, there is thick forest and bush so that we can not see through the bush. We have just arrived and are spreading out the tent when suddenly from in the air above the bush groups of impala are descending, landing on the dirt-track road, leaving the road, and ascending up and over the bush on the other side. They are coming in groups of three to four; and we can clearly see the still outline of their bodies when they are in the air; landing on the dirt-track road, a blur of motion when they are on the road; then still-photographs again, three-dimensional, floating up and over the bush on the other side.

They are appearing in the air above the thick bush, landing on the dirt-track road, then ascending over the bush on the other side; ten feet from we stand holding tent poles and stakes and we wait for the lion to come but nothing comes.

The Walls of Bolgatanga

"My. Look at that one."

"It was, I believe, near Zebila."

"Oh? They are splendid. Paul, do you see the one on the left?

"Magnificent. Absolutely."

"More wine?"

"Please."

The man who had been standing went into the kitchen and returned with the bottle and topped the glasses on the table as the two couples leaned back into the large sofa. The hum of the slide projector filled the room, which was dark, but for the light coming from the kitchen and the bright image filling the tall screen toward the wall.

There was the brilliant blue of sky at the top of the image and below the sky the curving brown, compound-walls of an African village with conical-shaped straw roofs; and covering the smooth mud walls from top to bottom in a riot of dark design were the painted geometrical shapes of angled lines and patterns. There were several naked children to one side smiling at the camera.

"Did they not wear clothes?" one of the women asked, looking at the screen.

"The children? Well, not there," said the host, standing. "It was a hundred degrees."

"Good god. A hundred?" said one of the men.

"The equator is not far. Just to the south."

"Good god. And this was where? Bolga...?"

"Around Bolgatanga. Almost to Upper Volta. This was the only area they painted the walls."

"Really?"

The host clicked the projector and another slide rotated onto the screen. Outside, the wind blew in the darkened street and swirls of snow occasionally passed across the light of the streetlamps.

On the sofa, the other woman, Maria, reached for the chip tray and dipped into the thick sauce. She picked up her wine glass and sipped, then held it in her hand as she leaned forward to look at the new image.

On the screen the sky was now gone and the brilliant patterns of a compound wall reflected brightly from close up; and they could clearly see the black paint of the angling lines against the soft-brown of the dwelling walls. From the corner, a small smiling face beamed up at the camera.

"Oh—how did he get in there?" Maria laughed.

"Look at this one," said the host, a returned Peace Corps Volunteer, and he rotated to the next slide. "—They are quick."

"Very," said Maria.

Now the sky was gone and so was the bottom of the painted wall where a small crowd of beaming children squeezed shoulder to shoulder into the frame. Only the very smallest stood naked, the others without shirts, but with shorts or short dresses.

"*Ha*—look at them, Paul," the first woman said to her husband, beside her. They had each pushed the sleeves of their sweaters up, finally warming in the heat of the house. Turtle necks rose up their necks from the sweaters.

"Now, how far from your school was this?" asked the tall, clean-shaven man, Paul; and he reached for the tray of hors d'oeuvres."

"Oh. A long ways," said the Peace Corps Volunteer. "I was very far to the south, near the coast. This was inland, two-hundred miles. More. You can see how barren the terrain has become. We're getting closer to the Sahara here."

"And this is where these painted walls were? The Sahara?"

"Well. It's still much further to the Sahara. But, yes, this area around Bolga. It's where the walls were. Everyone had talked about them. They were like nothing I saw anywhere else in Africa."

"Look at the children, Paul," said the first woman,

reaching over and resting her hand on her husband's arm.

"Did they have enough to eat?" said Paul.

"Well, there wasn't a lot of protein. But, yes, I think so."

He rotated to another slide. Now the walls were further back and people filled the entire foreground facing the camera. Adults had joined the children, young and old, and the smiles of what was now a small crowd extended from one side of the screen to the other.

"Did they mind you taking the photos?" said the other woman, Ann.

"No. Not really."

"Who's that on the right? He looks American," said Maria.

"With the beard? Oh, let me think. Arthur. He was another Peace Corps in the area."

"Really?"

"...Two hundred miles," said Paul. "You had traveled a long ways."

"Yeah, well, I had wanted to visit a friend at another school. Let me think. In Bawku. And see the walls. So, yes, a ways."

"It must have been difficult getting around."

"Brother—up there it was. I had almost been stranded at the friends. But, luckily, I got a ride... In fact...Arthur drove me...

"Oh?"

What the people in the living room could not see was the glare in the bearded man's eyes who was standing just to the side as I photographed the village of Zebila that morning in the blazing heat of the West African sun. Nor could they hear his voice. That day I had.

After visiting the friend, word came that the regular bus back to Bolga had been hired out for a funeral which meant only the infrequent and prohibitively expensive Peugeout taxis would be making the return run the next day when I wanted to leave. But, luckily, there was another Peace Corps Volunteer in the area, Arthur, who had a small pickup, and who would be making his once weekly stop at the friend's the next morning to drop off correspondence before driving on to Bolga.

Arthur was an African American who had been living alone for the last year and a half in a small village near Zebila, and before that with the other mostly white volunteers for the two months of training, and before that on the south side of Chicago where he had grown up in the 1950s and '60s.

He had agreed to the ride that morning, but for other reasons had not wanted to stop; but he knew about the walls and I convinced him it would only take a few minutes to get some photos. But when the people began crowding into the picture Arthur grew impatient, and then he became angry.

"Fuckin' African pictures. Like fuckin' National Geographic that all you white motherfuckers take back home and show all you other white motherfuckers your pictures of naked, mud-hut Africans. And it keeps

everybody thinking it's just a bunch of naked-ass savages humpin' around their mud-hut villages all day. Huntin' lions. Motherfucker."

I was stuck with Arthur for the ride back to Bolga, and he knew I was; but he also knew he would have to take me there, and he kept it up for the rest of the way, two more hours, as we sped down the empty highway over the baked, barren plains of northern Ghana. More often than the road, he faced me; his head turned ninety degrees on his shoulders, which were square to the wheel, the veins in his neck sometimes protruding; the black man from Chicago talking to the white kid from the suburbs.

"So, you were able to get around?" said the man on the sofa.

"Pretty much."

"It must have been difficult getting the photos," said the other man.

"It was. Very."

"Africa. So fascinating," said Maria. "If only someday, Paul, we could go."

"That would be quite something, wouldn't it?"

"More wine?" said the other woman, extending the bottle of Chianti toward the host.

"No thanks. I've had enough."

Miss Preston's Physics Class

Kodjo was the first to arise. The room was dark and only faintly could he see his younger brother and sister still asleep on mats on the clay floor. He had promised his mother he would bring fresh eggs from the Binto's house on the other side of the village so she could fry them before he went to school to take the examination. Stepping carefully so as not to awaken his siblings, he made his way to the bead-draped door and entered the main room of the house.

Kodjo's father arose next. He emerged from the room where Kodjo's parents slept on a bed, just as Kodjo opened the door to go to the street. Still awakening, his father waved a hand but did not speak; he crossed the room to where two farming cutlasses leaned against the wall, placing one of the cutlasses under his arm and holding the other in his hand. Slipping on his sandals, he left the house to go to his plot in the rainforest, where he would work until just before the sun went down.

Outside, as daylight spread across the hills and forests surrounding Oboso, Kodjo walked on the dirt-street toward the Binto's house. Everywhere now others were emerging from the mud-brick houses and Kodjo saw Lillian approaching with her two younger brothers, each with a metal bucket they would fill at the stream that ran beside the village.

"Wo ko osuo nnora? Nyami asleep o pa?" Lillian spoke to Kodjo in the village dialect, asking why God had not made the stream full last night, so she and her brothers would not have to wade to the middle.

"The air is not heavy, Lillian," Kodjo said in English. "The barometric pressure is high. The clouds with rain only come when the air is heavy."

"What are you speaking about, Kodjo?" Lillian said. "I think it is what they talk about at the school, in the upper forms. They teach you and make you smart. I wish I could go but my uncle's crops were only enough to send my older brother."

"Your uncle's crops are being wasted on your brother, Lillian: he doesn't know which end of the pencil to use. God grew the maize tall last year for you, Lillian. It would have been put to better use by someone as clever as you are. My father says the elders still talk of the math score you got in form one."

"It was so long ago, Kodjo. God will need fields of

maize to send these two first." Lillian put her arms around the shoulders of her two smaller brothers standing beside her with the empty buckets. Francis, the older, was smiling, and Kofi, the younger, was not. Francis couldn't wait to begin school; next year if the crop was big enough. Kofi cried whenever anyone mentioned him going to school; he did not want to be away from his house and mother.

Kodjo smiled. "Okay, Lillian, meko akoko. —I'm going for eggs. Bye-bye-o."

Kodjo turned and continued down the street as Lillian and her brothers left for the stream. As he approached the group of houses where the Binto's lived, he suddenly veered up the lane that led to the cement-block duplex beside the broken down water tower at the back of the village. On one side of the duplex lived Mr. Okah, the caretaker of the tower, and his family, and on the other side lived the white woman, Miss Preston, who taught science at the secondary school. In the yard in front of the house on the Okah's side, Mrs. Okah, wrapped in her colorful cloths, sat on a stool in front of a coal pot, stirring rice-meal for breakfast. Several chickens pecked in the short grass around her. She smiled and waved to Kodjo, who didn't wave back, who looked down; he did not want to bring attention to himself. On the other side of the duplex, where Miss Preston lived, the shutters were closed and there was no sign of life. She was either still asleep, Kodjo thought, or, more likely, had already left for the school.

Moving quickly, Kodjo turned down another street to continue on to the Binto's.

*   *   *

"O-jo-na pa-paa, Kodjo."

Kodjo walked in his school uniform past the group of men standing on the side of the road that led to the school. They had gathered beside the farmer, Kwaku Assim, who had a fresh bucket of palm wine he had just brought from a tree in the forest. Kodjo smiled and shifted the strap of his book bag from one shoulder to the other. It was his uncle, Anan, standing with the men and sipping wine from a gourd, who had spoken.

"Yo, wofa; medasi, paa," Kodjo said, thanking his uncle, who had told him he would do well on the examination.

His uncle, standing barefoot in shorts and a torn, red tee-shirt (which announced the Hoosiers of the University of Indiana in large letters across the front) took a drink from his gourd; he looked again at Kodjo. "The white woman," he said in English, "she has taught you to know the correct answers. You will score one hundred points!" His uncle laughed and drank some more.

Kodjo grinned; he waved goodbye to the men and continued down the road. When he got to the small market near the school he went to Mrs. Ketti's table where her daughter, Amma, stood with a platter of green oranges. Two of the oranges were cut in half, the moist pulp glistening in the morning sun. Kodjo went around the table and held Amma's hand; she grinned and swung Kodjo's arm. Letting go, Amma took a knife and cut one of the oranges in half, then picked up one of the previously cut halves, and, raising it into the air, squeezed the juice into her mouth. She held it up to Kodjo and squeezed the last into his mouth, tossing the remains onto the ground. Now she glanced around to make sure no one was looking, and, slowly, raised the short hemline of her dress upward to reveal the small panties with the tight, thin material that disappeared under her crotch. She smiled widely and watched Kodjo's eyes, transfixed downward, then raised the hemline a few inches more, revealing her navel and the smooth skin of her waist, before dropping the cloth.

She heard Kodjo groan.

Kodjo now took a step toward Amma, who, continuing to grin, took a step back. Kodjo took a longer step and Amma laughed and ran to the other side of the table. Kodjo ran the other way and grabbed her before she could get away and backed her up to one of the wood posts that supported the racks of palm fronds that provided shade for the tables. He held her hands and pushed his body against her. Amma laughed; she leaned up and roughly kissed Kodjo's mouth, who groaned again, returning the kiss.

A voice called out from the back of the shelter

where a group of women sat on low stools pealing tubers of yam: "*Amma, yen ko didi a paa.*"

Amma stepped back from Kodjo; she resumed swinging his arms. Without turning to look, she called to the women: "*Ani, ani, pa paa.*" She looked at Kodjo. "My mother needs me, she is preparing the soup for lunch."

Kodjo glanced over his shoulder and saw Mrs. Ketti, who smiled and waved. "*Asi ti test pa paa,*" Mrs. Ketti said, grinning, telling Kodjo to do well on the exam.

"*Yo, yedi Nyami asi,*" Kodjo called back, telling her he would do as well as God was willing." Now Kodjo looked at Amma and his expression became serious; he let go of one of her hands. "Did you talk to Francis?"

"Ani. He said no one came to her house, all of the weekend. That is four weekends running. Francis has seen no one. His brothers and sisters are watching, too. The white teacher that came last week with the car from Tarkaradi?—when it broke down?—he stayed at the home of the mechanic, Mr. Sheewa. Mr. Sheewa said she came to visit only once, during the day, but he was there all along. Kodjo, the white man did not go to stay at her house!" Amma poked Kodjo's chest with her finger. "*Not at all!*"

Kodjo looked away; he shook his head.

"Maybe they are different," Amma said. "Maybe the white body, the brain. The way they are. Different."

Looking off through the market, Kodjo let go of Amma's hand. "No. I don't believe this. There must be someone. Someone must come. Late at night. Or she goes somewhere. She meets with someone. A secret place. During the day. A house. A hut. Maybe in the forest."

"Dabi, dabi, dabi pa paa!" Amma looked deridingly at Kodjo. "She does not go in the forest. *I see her every day!* She passes by. You know this. Four months she has been in Oboso. She goes with the bursar on the school bus to Tarkwa, on every Friday. For the cow meat. But Yaa and her sister go as well. She buys the meat. She goes to the chop bar for the rabbit soup, and a bottle of beer—if they are having any. She comes back on the bus and goes to her house. Before the sun goes down behind the ridge."

Kodjo thought of the earth spinning on its axis, of the ridge rising up to block the sun, of the shadow that brings the night, like Miss Preston had taught them in her class. He thought of how the rays of the sun came through the atmosphere from straight above and seemed to strike Oboso, and the rainforest around Oboso, at the equator, the same way everyday, for the whole of the year. But in the land where Miss Preston was from—USA—it was not the same. She showed them how the angle changed as the earth, tilted on its axis, rotated around the sun. She said that for half of the year the air became cold.

"There is no one, Kodjo!" Amma said at the table in the market, taking one of Kodjo's hands again.

"Everyone has looked. Everyone has watched. No one has seen anyone. No one comes to her house. She doesn't go to anyone's house."

Kodjo took Amma's other hand. "I don't know how this can be. She will answer all the questions. In all the books. Even those Aslan's brother brings from university. We have showed them to her. She knows all. This physics! —*University!*" He looked off through the market.

Letting go of Kodjo's hands, Amma leaned over and rested her elbows on the table; she cradled her face in her palms. "How can she know this much? The maths. The physics. I don't know them. Fail, fail, fail. They hurt my brain. This thing: forces, atoms. I'm not learning them. They are too difficult. I am a woman. I don't know these things. How can she know them? Everyday she knows them. She is keeping this thing, the knowledge, in her brain. But four months. She lives in Oboso alone. Where is the man? —I'm not seeing him!"

Kodjo shook his head. "Owusula is saying he will find out. He is saying he will ask her. Directly. Ocran and Ebin will join him. After the examination. They are saying they will go with Owusula. I will go, too. I will join them. We will find out.

"Maybe the man is invisible. Maybe they can do this: the invisible. They are very smart."

"No—*Amma!*" Kodjo said, cringing as though he had bitten into something sour. "Don't insult us. ...Invisible man..." He shook his head.

"But I have heard of this: the invisible man. Kwami's brother has a book, from America. It is about him. He can't be seen."

"It is fantasy—make believe!"

Leaning over further, Amma rested her arms on the table and lay her head down. "*You* make believe. My mother says all the chiefs of Oboso, who have ever lived, they are all still in the ancient trees, and come to the palace. The chief confers with them on important matters—*they* are invisible."

Kodjo shook his head again. He thought of what Miss Preston had taught them about light particles, how they came from the sun and bounced off all matter, then entered the eye and stimulated the brain. She said this was how we see things, what made things visible.

Kodjo looked at Amma: "We will ask her. Today. After the exam." His face cringed again. "The very exam that *she* has written! —*Physics! Form five!*"

Amma shifted her head on her arms; she yawned and looked up at Kodjo. "She should be like your uncle. She should be stupid, like him. It is because he has no woman. No wonder he drinks the wine."

Looking off into the market, which was empty but for the women in back and a few others at the small tables, Kodjo reached down and pulled Amma up. He wrapped his arms around her and she laid her cheek against his chest. "Okay," Kodjo said, "The exam. I am going. Me ko school." He kissed her forehead and left the table.

In the deep shade of the palm fronds, Amma watched as Kodjo made his way out of the market and disappeared down the road. She reached down and took some oranges from a bag on the ground and placed them on the table. "*Yeeaazz, oranges, oranges,*" she called out to whoever might hear.

*   *   *

The students were gathered in front of the classrooms, talking loudly, when Kodjo came up the road to the school in the morning sun. He saw Owusula and Ebin near the science room, talking to Nana and Justine, two girls from form four. Owusula had been with Justine for all of the school term, and Kodjo was sure he had been with her alone. Owusula had always been the smartest in the class; even back in elementary school his hand had been the first to rise. Now, in secondary, his scores on the examinations were the highest; it was no surprise, he studied harder than anyone, and he had been with many of the girls. And Justine, his new girlfriend, who the year before had barely made it out of form three, was now getting excellent marks amongst the girls, although it seemed she rarely studied.

Waving to Owusula and Ebin, who waved in return, Kodjo thought of Amma. He liked what they did alone, but, still, she hardly ever went to school anymore; she hadn't received a passing grade in a year. Now she spent all day selling oranges at her mothers table in the market by the school. He thought of how he spent most of his free time with her, often just the two of them. He thought she should be smarter.

On the second floor of the main building block, Kodjo saw Miss Preston, in one of the knee-length, sleeve-less jumpers she seemed always to be wearing, standing on the outdoor veranda with Mr. Adwele, the Assistant Headmaster, and several other teachers. They were talking and laughing, as they seemed always to be doing when they were not standing in a classroom at a blackboard with a piece of chalk in their hand. He could see Miss Preston, it seemed, from a mile away; the shocking white skin widening the eyes of all within sight: standing at a table in the village market, examining produce; looking out the window from within a packed bus; walking along a village street with twenty children crowded around, trying to touch her arm, following her like chicks scampering around a mother hen. She goes left, they go left; she goes right, they go right; she stops to examine an onion, they punch each other to stand closest.

Up on the veranda, Miss Preston, laughing hard, put her hand on Mr. Adwele's shoulder; she bent over, dropping her head, seeming about to faint from laughter. Mr. Adwele, grinning, was saying something, the other teachers beside them also laughing. Mr. Adwele was from the village. A successful native of Oboso, he had excelled at the school, gone to the university, and now, back home, was the assistant headmaster. His wife and children lived in a house near Kodjo's family.

From down the veranda, wearing his black horn-rimmed glasses and carrying a briefcase, came Mr. Asim, the economics teacher. Kodjo saw Miss Preston and the others turn to greet him. He watched carefully how she and Mr. Asim interacted, but saw nothing unusual. Mr. Asim, from the distant port city of Tema—where his wife and children lived—slept with some of the form five girls, everyone knew. So did a few of the other teachers. They practiced *Obolo,* a way to keep the mind and body healthy. At first Miss Preston complained bitterly, until Mr. Adwele threatened to transfer her, then she found other concerns on which to focus where progress seemed more likely. Such as the lack of books and science supplies, and the minimal amounts of protein the school kitchen served to the students.

Oboso Secondary was a rural school; the local girls, from farming families, would eventually settle into a domestic life with a local farmer. Mr. Asim, assigned to the school by the Education Administration, as were most of the other teachers, could practice *Obolo* and possibly find a second wife, preferably with a large farm. Throughout the valley, most all revenue was from produce sold at market.

Kodjo and Owusula did not like Mr. Asim; he was strict with the boys, less so with the girls. Especially

Christina Ekow, the most beautiful girl in the school. The year before, soon after Mr. Asim arrived, Christina began receiving high marks on the exams and was promoted to form five. This, despite not even pretending to know the first thing about any subject. No one had ever heard her speak in class. Christina was from the village, but her father, Mr. Ekow, who ran the local logging operation, was wealthy; he owned the only private automobile in the valley. In the village they called him the cash register.

Of course, Christina had also been promoted in the years before Mr. Asim arrived; her father was friendly with many of the business managers in Tarkwa, the regional trading center to the west of Oboso. He was particularly friendly with the beverage distributor, who kept him supplied with beer. Mr. Ekow then supplied Mr. Adwele, the Assistant Headmaster; Christina and her siblings advanced each year, and all were happy.

Kodjo watched Mr. Asim on the veranda as he stepped in between Mr. Adwele and Miss Preston—his back now to Miss Preston—to have a word with Mr. Adwele. Everyone's laughter seemed to abate, Miss Preston lingering for a moment, then walking off down the veranda with the other teachers and disappearing into the vacant classroom that was used as the teachers lounge. On the veranda, Mr. Asim and Mr. Adwele continued to talk.

"Kodjo Dinkins, are your pencils sharp?"

Kodjo turned to see Christina Ekow walking up

the grass with Melody Burkma. Christina was wearing her bright new *Nike* running shoes that her father had purchased for her on a recent trip to Great Britain. The shoes were worth more than the entire wardrobes of the families of each of the other students in all the schools of the valley.

Christina had addressed Kodjo by his nickname, *Dinkins*, passed on from middle school, where nicknames blossomed onto all the students.

"Ani, Farrah, a-a-prepare-o paa," Kodjo said to Christina, calling her *Farrah*, from the American TV star, *Farrah Fawcett*. "I am ready, Christina, are you?"

Christina, clutching her book bag, looked at Kodjo. "...Physics?" She shook her head. "I will go. I will look at these questions. I will write..." She glanced up to the veranda where Mr. Asim and Mr. Adwele continued to converse. "I will see what happens."

Kodjo looked at Christina, up to the veranda, back to Christina. "You will do fine, Farah Fawcett Majors. The answers will appear...like the colors of the rainbow."

Christina looked at the sky as though searching for rain clouds. She looked back to Kodjo. "Miss Preston is concerned. She has been tutoring me and Melody all of the week—oh, I'm telling you, Dinkins, we have seen *no* one—but she says our maths is poor. She says without the maths, we cannot know the physics. Is this true, Dinkins?"

Standing on the grass in front of the main school

block, Kodjo squinted in the morning sun, which had risen to its high place directly overhead. To one side of the village much of the forest had been logged by Christina's father—the massive hardwoods hauled to Tema and then shipped to the far corners of the Earth—but on the other side rose the ancient trees, where the spirits of Oboso had resided for eternity: a lush, green tropical foliage through which the towering white trunks of the hardwoods rose toward the heavens.

"Miss Preston is the smartest person to have ever lived in Oboso," Kodjo began to Christina and Melody at the front of the school, "—how she must miss her home. She has been to university in States. There they learn the answers. But I think she is living here alone. So it is a mystery how she is able to still know these things. ...You said you saw no one?"

Both Christina and Melody shook their heads.

Kodjo thought for a moment. "But it is true about the maths. It is the blood of the physics. Without it the physics can not be."

"Then my physics will die, Dinkins," Christina said. "But Melody will survive, she has been understanding more."

Melody squinted in the sun. "Miss Preston has been coming to my house. My brother has also helped. With the grace of God I will know the answers."

"Okay, Dinkins, we are going to the classroom."

Christina looked for a moment at Kodjo. "I will be sitting beside Owusula... He will help me."

A look of concern passed over Kodjo's face; he turned briefly toward the ancient trees and summoned his deepest resolve. "...I think Owusula will be helping Justine."

Christina shot a look at Kodjo—like the spears the ancestors had used against the white slaving parties—that softened Kodjo's initial impulse. "He will help me—as well." She stared for a long moment, then slowly turned and walked confidently away in her new shoes. Melody followed.

*   *   *

"Quiet, please...quiet." Miss Preston stood before the twenty-five students of form-five physics with a large stack of stapled, legal-length, mimeographed papers. "Josephine...time to sit...Josephine."

Bright sunlight poured in through the windows along one side of the classroom; outside, a low tangle of jungle, ablaze in yellows and greens, reached like a hand from the base of the forest into the clearing where the school had been built.

"You will have ninety minutes to complete the exam," Miss Preston continued at the head of the class, order gradually spreading throughout the rows of desks, the hushed, final-snaps of irritated voices echoing in the room.

Near the front, on one side, Owusula sat upright

in his chair, three pencils and two erasers aligned on his bare desk, his expression, clear and alert, fixed on Miss Preston. Beside him sat Justine, looking slightly dazed, like the young gazelles that sometimes emerged from the newly logged forest. On the other side sat Christina, looking as though this was the last place in all the world she wanted to be. She inspected her shoes to see how they were doing.

On the other side of the classroom sat Kodjo, with Ocran on one side, and Ebin on the other. They shifted in their seats, moved their pencils and erasers around, stretched their necks, listened to Miss Preston.

"Please read the questions carefully before you place a mark—I'll hand out additional paper for your calculations." Miss Preston looked around the classroom. "And take your time. But try to write something, even if you don't know the answer. —Guess." There was a brief discussion amongst the students as to the meaning of the word *guess*. "When you're finished, bring your papers to the front. And please, no talking during the exam." Miss Preston, dressed for exam day in an African-print blouse and knee-length skirt, smiled at her class. On her feet were the remains of thread-bare leather sandals; her auburn hair wrapped in a bun behind her head and held with two ivory clips; tiny elephant-shaped earrings dangled at the sides of her face.

Now there were a few final murmurings amongst the students, the loudest coming from Christina.

"Did you have a question, Christina?" Miss Preston, smile remaining, earrings dangling, looked at Christina sitting beside Owusula.

"I'm hungry, Miss Preston."

"Oh, Christina, I'm sorry. I'm sure the kitchen will be having a big lunch, right after the exam."

At the home of her father, the cash register—where she would visit as often as possible—Christina ate more than anyone in the valley. More even than what Miss Preston, from the richest country on Earth, was able to secure. But at the school she had to eat whatever the kitchen was serving: often a small fish-head with just a little rice.

Christina looked briefly out the windows; she twisted her pencil in her hand, said something quickly in dialect to Owusula.

Everyone looked at Miss Preston's sandals, then at Christina's shoes.

"Okay, let's start," said Miss Preston, and she carried the stack of exams over to the row of students beside the windows and began to count them out.

*   *   *

Ocran was the first to arise. He carried his papers up to the table where Miss Preston had been silently sitting, trance-like, for over an hour, looking off through the open windows toward the forest. She turned to Ocran, still dream-like, then straightened in her chair and took his papers, separating the calculations from the exam.

Melody arose next. She gathered her papers and notebooks and came to the table, handing the papers to Miss Preston. "Very hard," she said with a pained expression. Miss Preston didn't reply and Melody followed Ocran to the door and out into the bright sun of the late-morning.

Slowly, more students began to rise, gathering their possessions and bringing their exams up to the table, then filing out the door.

Christina came up—Owusula still writing away at his desk. She separated her papers, handing Miss Preston her exam. "I'm not understanding this—" She flipped the exam to the second page and pointed to a question in the middle of the page. There was a small sketch Miss Preston had made of three cows standing on the back of a truck with the springs of the truck compressed. It was apparent why Miss Preston taught physics and not art.

"Opposing forces," Miss Preston said.

Christina twisted her head for a better look. She pointed to her answer. "Correct?"

Miss Preston smiled; she checked her wristwatch and stood and looked out at the class. "Five more minutes, everyone. It's time to finish up..." She looked again at Christina, who slowly turned and walked toward the door. "...Guess at any of the multiple choice you haven't done..."

Now people began talking—hushed arguments

breaking out throughout the room—and most of the class arose, en mass, and made its way to the front and out the door. The students who remained, either hunched over their desks and writing, or leaning back and gazing out into nothingness.

Miss Preston checked her watch again, took a step forward. "Okay, times up...Kodjo, Owusula..."

With a final check, Kodjo and Owusula, along with Ebin, brought their exams to the front. As they returned to their seats to collect their belongings, they began arguing loudly in dialect.

The argument grew as they made their way to the door, Miss Preston looking up as she gathered the exams at the table. "Everything okay?" she called to the boys, who didn't respond, who continued to converse loudly as they went out the door.

Now Miss Preston could hear a commotion outside—the sound of a large group of people, of a crowd. And through the open door and the windows along the wall, she saw what looked like most of the class gathered on the grass outside.

She put all the exams and papers and the rest of her books into her large carrying bag and went to the door. As she stood in the doorway, she looked out to see the entire class gathered on the grass, everyone turning toward her, Owusula, Kodjo, Ocran and Ebin, at the front, waving at everyone to be quiet.

Miss Preston slowly crossed the grass to where her class was gathered in the late-morning sun. Now she saw others from the village standing behind and to the sides: Amma, whom she rarely saw at the school anymore, who was usually selling oranges at the small market before the school, whom she thought was Kodjo's girlfriend; Lillian, whom she knew from Lillian's brother in the English class Miss Preston sometimes helped in; Mr. Okah, the water-tower attendant, who lived in the other half of the cement duplex, who spoke almost no English, whom she rarely saw.

Miss Preston looked out at the sea of eyes fixed on her, now a few students from other classes slowly approaching from the sides, along with some of the school staff and a few other teachers. At the back, Christina stood restlessly, examining her fingernails. Beside her, in his black horn-rimmed glasses, stood Mr. Asim.

As everyone grew quiet, Owusula, Kodjo, Ocran, and Ebin, each took a step forward. Owusula and Ocran took another. Then Owusula took one more.

Standing before Miss Preston in the blazing heat of the West African sun, his forehead arced with beads of sweat, Owusula cleared his voice. Then he addressed the white woman.

"Miss Preston, you are our teacher of the physics and the maths—we thank you for the great sacrifice you have made to come to Oboso from your home. It is known that these, along with the other sciences, are the most difficult subjects in all the Education Services. In the upper forms—four and five—they can only be learned by the brightest mind. The trained and alert mind. The mind with the highest capacity of the mental reasonings. The mind that is capable of accessing with—what's this?—analytical accuracy, the tallest blocks of the physics and maths chambers. Miss Preston, you are knowing all these things. We, the students of Oboso Secondary, see the extent of your mind...and yet...we do not know how this can be. "

Owusula briefly looked back to Kodjo and Ocran. Clearing his throat, he again turned to Miss Preston. A loud cough came from Christina at the back. Mr. Asim looked off toward the forest. "...Miss Preston, with the spirit of Oboso listening..." many in the crowd turned to where the ancient trees rose up through the green foliage. "Miss Preston...we must know—we *demand* to know—who...who, Miss Preston...who is it you are doing this thing: having with the sexual relations of the body?"

As the heat waves rose in ripples from both the organic and non-organic surfaces of the valley of Oboso, breaking the otherwise silence, came a loud thump.

It was the thump of a heavy bag striking the ground. And, leaping forward, Owusula and Ocran caught Miss Preston—the earrings dangling like Richter needles in a massive quake—timbering toward them—like one of the trees logged in the forest—the moment before she hit the earth.

Around Accra

If you are there at either of the rest houses, the Presbyterian or Evangelical, then you can start off out of the confusion, in the quiet of an old building set back within one of the large shady rest house compounds, and, if you already have the food, make your own breakfast in one of the large old rest house kitchens, which are well stocked with cooking utensils, as well as with gas stove and refrigerator.

So you can drink your cup of Nescafe' with sugar and eat your bread, and maybe fry an egg; and in the early morning in the pleasant rest house dining room with the large overhead ceiling fan already on—the always thick humid air circulating slowly throughout the large room and not yet hot, and the bright sunlight coming through the tall windows—the crows of the roosters and chickens and the calls of the people outside in awakening-Accra can be heard, but are few, as few of either live within the walls of the old rest house compounds; and in the pleasant dining room other travelers may come down for coffee and food, also.

But you have not come to Accra to sit in one of the pleasant old rest house dining-rooms—although if you have been out in the bush for several months without electricity or pipe-born water it would be a legitimate goal—but to buy supplies and run errands, and to be in Accra, the large West African city, and revitalize your bush-worn soul.

So with your light, cloth shoulder-bag, and wearing sandals and a light, cotton shirt and pants, and with a general plan of where you will be going and how you will get there, you set out on foot from the rest house; and already outside the tropical sun is high enough to be striking you from above the tall cluster of trees within the compound, and the air is damp and hot, and the sounds of the people calling to each other from amongst the small cement houses outside the compound walls are more frequent, and louder, as are the cawing of the roosters and chickens running about on the ground between the houses. And this time you are going first to the three-story, G.N.T.C. department store across from the large open-air Makola Market in the heart of the trading area to look for canned foods, and, walking the three blocks along the shady, cement-house-lined residential street with the tall oaks and the shorter palms rising above the houses to busy Cantoments Road, you begin to sense the increasing masses of people who congregate more densely around the main arterials of the city and to encounter the many small children living in the houses along the street who, upon seeing a strange European on foot, call out loudly to you. And reaching paved Cantoments, which is noisy and busy with a solid flow of cars and trucks bouncing along the pot-holed, two-lane street on their way into the center of the city, and lined with the many smaller stores of the residential outskirts—including a few American-looking gas stations—and with many brightly-clad local women selling hot foods and various merchandise from small wood tables and kiosks lining the tree-shaded street—and, also, strong with the smell of the open sewers—you begin trying to flag down one of the many taxis that are roaring past in the thick traffic as you walk in the flow of people beside one of the sewers bordering the street. But the first taxis are full, so you can try hitching, which is a good way to get around Accra if you are alone or with just one other person, because there are many wealthy people driving about in very nice Peugeots and Mercedes and they do not like to see a European walking in the crowds and heat. But, usually, before you must walk very far on increasingly busy and warm Cantoments, one of the old battered Datsun taxis moving quickly along the rough street on its way into central Accra that is only packed very full will stop and let you either squeeze into the front passenger bucket-seat with the other passenger who is already there, or into the small backseat bench with the three other passengers who already back there, and, sitting half on an office worker's lap and half wedged up against a door, the jam-packed taxi with the sleepy, eyes-diverting, half-smiling people—smiling, now that their day has begun with a strange, Accra-walking European pressed up against them—pulls out into the rushing traffic of Cantoments and heads for the center of Accra, two miles away, where the massive central Makola Market is located and the main banks and office buildings and the large government-run department stores, and, also, the thickest crowds; and although you have only walked a short distance and it is still the early morning, the back of your shirt is already soaked through with sweat from the damp heat.

But the drive into central Accra on Cantoments is a good one, especially in the morning, because just beyond the large, newly-constructed open-air soccer stadium, where the pleasant Cantoments neighborhood ends and the newer government buildings begin at the edge of central Accra, the road swings south for several blocks and there are no houses or buildings to obstruct the southerly view, and, coming up suddenly in the bright morning sunlight a few hundred yards in front is the wide, blue, white-capped Atlantic, stretching away to each side and off into the horizon; and riding in the crowded taxi and looking out over the swell-covered water it is best to start the day by having the feeling that comes from seeing the ocean, and trying, if you can, to go out there for a moment, because it will soon be very difficult to have that pleasant feeling when you are closed in on a thickly-crowded street and there is quite a large amount of garbage nearby and the people are sitting near it. No, you would not want to sit near it; but it is hard to keep walking for more than eight hours in crowded Accra so you should at least try to have a good book.

So you are lucky if you get to see the ocean before being dropped off in the center of Accra; which is what has now happened after your car turned onto High street and came back toward the center of the city and stopped at the dust-stirred central taxi-station across from jammed Makola Market in the vehicle-and-people-packed central commercial area. And paying the driver the reasonable four cedi fare and stepping out into the thick crowd of traders and buyers and workers, who are coming and going in all directions, you begin to move quickly with the flow of the crowd and do not stop, and try to look very much as though you know where you are going, and what you are doing, because whereas a moment before you were the center of attention in a taxi of five, now you are the center of attention in a crowd of thousands. But you actually do not know for sure which route you will take to the G.N.T.C. department store, but try to look as though you do, so that as every bare-foot child and colorfully-clad market woman, and every old man, turns to stare grinning at you, and calls out loudly to you with a local word, you are not uncertain or self-conscious or sensitive enough to stop, or respond, or listen, like you did when you first arrived in the region and the calling out quickly ate away at you and you were exhausted thirty minutes into the crowd; and then sometimes comes the confusion: especially in the heat. But to get done now what you want to get done you are planning on eight hours, not thirty minutes, and so keep moving and only partly see and hear the callers. But you do know they are all looking at you; it is just something you can't help but see; and you do hear them and you know you are quite a sight and it is difficult to not let it get to you and eat away at you: like when you are in the thickest of Accra crowds on a hot loud street near the twenty-block-long Makola Market and the bright sunlit street is jammed with hawkers and the market-women who seemingly live at their wood stalls and your light clothing is soaked through from the heat and the smell of the open-sewers hangs thickly in the humid air. And the crowd spills out from the broken cement of the sidewalk into the car-jammed street and they all call out to you and point to you and laugh out at you, and stare long at you, and their skin is of the blackest black and you are weak and awkward and they see that you are awkward and this makes them laugh harder and to feel very sorry for you because you are so awkward; and word that you are coming passes quickly through the crowd just ahead and doorways fill up and wood-shuttered windows open and the smallest children reach out in awe to touch, and you are trying to be serious and to look as though you do not notice them and know where you are going and are not bothered; but it does eat away at you and wear you down no matter how many times before you have been to Accra. But it is also what is so very exciting and exhilarating, and brings you back to life, and why you have come out of the bush and to Accra in the first place, and you would not trade it for any other experience in the world; but it can be easy to think of the wide ocean.

But being used enough to the crowds, and liking the aliveness of the packed commercial area, and glad to be where you can finally take care of some of the errands that you have been waiting three months in the deep bush to take care of, that you can only take care of in the capital city, today you laugh back and smile back, and talk back in some of the local dialect that you have slowly over the months learned to speak, and which makes the heavy-set market women cry out in glorious surprise and embarrassment; and moving down Selwyn Street in the bright morning sunlight from the dust-stirred taxi-drop in front of the loud central market, you cross the crowded street, dodging in between the endless flow of automobiles and buses, and the bouncing vans and brightly-painted trucks, all packed full on the inside with people and bulging on the outside with large wooden boxes and heavy cotton sacks of various goods that are strapped high onto the flat tops and to the backs of the vehicles; and you try to think again about what you hope to get done today in Accra. And now seeing back across the street amongst the white, humidity-stained two and three-story cement buildings with the corrugated metal roofs the busy central Accra Post Office, where there is the best chance of finding the small blue areo-gram postal letters that are difficult to find out of Accra but are your best means of getting a letter out of the region, you decide to forget for now about going to the G.N.T.C. department store, which is the rest of the way down Selwyn, and, instead, decide to try to get the areo-grams. And having run out of them two months before and not having been able to send a letter since that you knew for sure would make it out of the country; and having re-crossed jammed Selwyn and entered the crowded building and now seeing the smiling but serious Western-dressed, male-African clerk behind the counter bring out a handful of the letters from a drawer—the clerk who moments before, having seen you standing within the loud confusion of the hot, packed inner-lobby, came out from behind his window and led you to the front of the long line: not to the disappointment of those in the line, but to their strongest approval, because they feel very sorry for a weak, awkward European standing in a large crowd of local people, and they do not like to see a weak European having to stand and suffer in a long hot line—and now having the precious areo-grams in your hand, you feel the aliveness grow, and having been successful with this part of Accra the aliveness of the crowd seeps into you, and it is a feeling that makes you glad; but had you failed the crowd would have taken the life out of you and you would have had to think of the ocean.

But you have the letters and are feeling good about that, and you have the aliveness of Accra now, and the sense that the journey into crowded Accra has been worth it even if you get nothing else done (now that you know that you can communicate with the outside world again) and it is only mid-morning and outside the burning sun is beating down hard onto the alive and dead crowd. So knowing how worth it this has been: coming through the Accra crowds to the central post office and finding the areo-grams, you decide to locate one of the small, local coffee and food shops of central Accra to sit and eat a mid-morning pastry and drink another cup of coffee, and be among the local people in a pleasant, out-of-the-way, coffee-bar type of shop.

And remembering the small food bar off the dirt ally behind Okaeti Lane in the middle of the garment district only three blocks away, you set off through the thick crowd on a side street off Selwyn with your now areo-gram-full shoulder-bag for the small, single-story cement and wood shops of the garment district where you hope to again find the small coffee shop that had saved you once before in Accra when you had failed; and while in the garment district you can look at the many fine *Eve'* dresses, one of which, with the intricate embroidery around the neck and down the front, you know you must buy for a woman back home, be she your wife or girlfriend or mother or sister, before you leave alive West Africa for good, because to not bring back one of the floor length, tie-dyed, brightly-patterned dresses from the alive garment district of Accra to a woman back home in America who would not have liked the heat and wonders why you left in the first place, would be a disgrace to your sense of taste and to your knowledge of what these American women appreciate and like. And a tie-dyed *Eve'* dress from West Africa an educated American woman would like very much, and appreciate very much, and be very aware of from whom it came and not forget later.

So moving down the very narrow back street that is bordered on each side by small open sewers and, beyond, the walls of the lower cement buildings of the area, and with only one lane open for the flow of the smaller sized vehicles that could make the tight turn onto the narrow street and the other lane bumper to bumper with parked vehicles that have been used to deliver the many sacks of yams and cassava and rice, and the cases of canned milk and mackerel and radio batteries, and the piles of cloth and clothing that flow endlessly into central Accra, you come through the smaller, head-turning crowd of the back street and out suddenly to wide and jammed Liberty Avenue that in the mid-morning heat has become a loud mass of traders and hawkers and workers, sitting and standing and walking, and of cars and trucks and buses roaring by on the inner lanes and crawling or stopped or broken down on the curb lanes; and dodging through the traffic you cross to the other side and then try quickly to remember the way to the food bar so that you will not have to stop which will attract an audience that may want to touch. And seeing Okaitei Lane at the edge of the Accra train station, where the baking black soot of the dirt beneath the tracks leading off from the station heats the air above into rippling waves and the edge of the metal shacks in the distance at the back of the station, and the rising smoke from the cooking fires amongst the shacks, can be vaguely seen through the heat waves, you turn onto the lane and move again amongst a smaller crowd through the maze of narrow back streets and alleys lined with open-air wood-structured shops that are draped heavily with clothing and brightly patterned cloth, and more clothing and racks of inexpensive shoes, and still more cloth; and moving down another dirt lane you come now to a group of low cement buildings with store-fronts at the street level and between two of the long, narrow textile stores, with male tailors busily sewing at foot-powered machines at the backs of the stores, is the small coffee shop that you had come upon once before.

And inside it is clean by Accra standards and there are cups of instant Nescafe', which is much better than the low-grade, locally grown coffee, and which may be taken with sugar and milk and small home-baked, meat-pies, and there are tables and chairs and only a few people, and, ordering the coffee and the meat pastry, you sit in the bright sunlight near the open window and begin to drink the coffee as, overhead, the large ceiling-fan blows the warm damp air about.

Yes, it is pleasant looking out the window to the people on the street (some of whom are looking back) and as the coffee and sugar spread throughout your body, you can relax and remember the ocean and what she will think, you hope, about the fine dress. That is if, by now, she is not married, or something, or maybe shacking up with some other man, or something like that, that you, 8,000 miles away in a small coffee shop in Accra, would have a difficult time having much to say about. So, still looking out the open window, you think instead about the open sewers and the irony of that. The open sewers? Such irony, you think. You came here to learn, and to be alive, and one of the main things you end up learning about is the extremeness of the open sewers of Accra. You were not expecting that. But you get use to it; but not really, and definitely at no time during the first six months. You try not to look at them, though; but it is dangerous at night. They are built of cement in the cities, and are about two feet wide and three to four feet deep, and they line every street and every road in all of West Africa and it is probably a good thing. Something has to happen to it. But is it not a lot that while you are standing on a busy street in alive Accra at an open-air shop of very fine *Adrinkra* dresses; and the very pretty and very dark-skinned *Ashanti* girl who is wearing one of the brightly patterned dresses is quietly helping you to look through the long rack, that there, just three short feet behind you, is a wide one? And it is hot, very hot; and that does little to squander the strong smell. Very little. In fact, I may as well say it: it makes it worse. But, really, if you are in Accra and succeeding with you errands you forget about the sewers; usually. Unless you had once fallen into one and then the memory is always there. But that is not necessarily something you would want others to be aware of; it is not necessarily something you would want to let out. Having fallen into an Accra sewer is a personal thing; but it was sure unpleasant the night it happened. But, you see, I really don't want to talk about it all that much, because I really don't know you all that well. But it was the most bizarre experience and I wasn't at all expecting it to happen when it did. I had seen it happen to others several times over the months, and there was no predicting it; but it happened most often at night when it was difficult to see and the man or the woman was a little drunk, or as in the case of Ted, very drunk, but Ted was always very drunk and he was always falling into Accra sewers so we really won't count drunk-Ted. But it happened to other people, also, and when it would happen it caught everyone by surprise; especially the faller. And it is very embarrassing. There you are, several men and women friends, returning at night from an excellent meal out, taken with several bottles of fine beer, and feeling very good about things and talking a lot and feeling good from the beer, and relaxing, and maybe one of the men is liking one of the women and it may be that the woman is glad about that and is liking the man also, and you are pleasantly strolling along the dark city street and there are four of you strolling and then—whoops—now there are only three. One of the men has dropped into a sewer. And, believe me, it changes everything; but they are not very deep and I never saw anyone not land on his or her feet, and then quickly, by-the-grace-of-God, quickly, the faller is up and out of the shallow, cement ditch practically before they had time to touch bottom. And I never saw anyone injured more than a scrape on the leg, and nothing more than get their feet wet; but still it changes everything. You have now fallen into an Accra sewer. You are not hurt, but no one really knows what to say and you are scared. You never ever thought that it would happen to you; and you have to wait until back at the rest house to clean up. And later you don't know what to say about it; but it changes you: you lose some of your idealism, and you view the world differently. And you are quieter, now, also. For quite some time, quieter. You may also forget about the girl.

But you can not sit in a coffee shop for all of a

warm Accra morning thinking about some of the unexpected things that have happened to you in this very different part of the world, so, finishing the cup of coffee and getting up from the table, you go back out into the crowd, and, so as not to arrive before it becomes hot-hot: like from the thick humid heat that will come in the mid-afternoon, you begin to head for the open-air Makola Market in the center of the commercial district, which is usually one's main destination when coming to Accra.

Oh, to God; Makola. I am thinking of a word that, if you were told you must describe Makola with but a single word, is the word that you would choose. Ready? Big. That is the word. Very big; and crowded. Oh, God; Makola. It is roughly the shape of a great rectangle extending for many blocks in each direction directly in the center of the city, and it is filled with dust and dirt and the thickest crowds and it is large; I'm telling you: very large; and crowded. Oh; Makola: you enter into one of its narrow corridors from off one of the many busy streets that surrounds it, but you think first before you go in; yes, you think first a lot. And it is crowded and dirty, but alive: by the grace-of-God, it is very alive.

So moving again through the garment district the several blocks back to the packed alive crowd at the edge of Makola, you try and think of exactly where in the blocks-long market the precious tins of milk and Nescafe' and margarine are most likely to be found, and, seeing a brief opening in one of the narrow crowded, stall-lined corridors leading into the market, you plunge into the deafening chaos of tightly packed bodies and blocks-long rows of food-and-merchandise-filled, wood-stalls and kiosks, and the tall shed-like structures with the corrugated metal roofs to protect the high stacks from the hot sun, and in May and September the rains. And sitting heavily on low stools, the large market women with their thick wads of cash who run the local economy and their many daughters at their sides who are learning to sell, and everywhere surrounding the stalls loud hordes of playing children; and they all call out to you over the high roar of the loud market chatter.

And moving deeper into the noisy sea of tightly-packed bodies, you ask one of the sellers in the local dialect where there is margarine being sold; and the heavy-set woman may send a small-boy to guide you to the precious tins which are difficult to find and sold only at the very high black-market prices; except for when the government cracks down on the feared *Kalibuli* traders and stops the flow of Western-made goods out of the country and floods the market with the precious canned foods. But, really, it does not matter to you if you have to pay the *Kalibuli* man's high prices, because you are a rich foreigner with access to the treasured American currency and will pay gladly for one of the rare tins of margarine, or a jar of the delicious Nescafe' coffee. And coming up a loud, jammed, market corridor in the heat of the noon-time sun with the barefoot small-boy who has been sent to show you where the margarine is being sold today, you see now, displayed amongst a long, tightly-packed food-section at the back of several connected stalls, one of the neatly stacked pyramids of the large yellow cans of the Western-made margarine that you will treasure for weeks back home in the small kitchen of the house where you live, and, begging sincerely in the hot sun, try to get the now-standing woman behind the table in the stall to come down with her very high black market price. But it is difficult trying to bargain with the colorfully-clad madam because of the crowd of small children gathered behind who are trying to touch the skin on the backs of your arms and the loud shouting and laughter of the bargaining from the tables nearby and the strong smell of the sewers and the flies trying to land wherever there is bare skin. But the Madam likes you very much for having come a great distance into Makola and for having such light skin and a very long thin nose, and for being at her stall which is now drawing a large crowd: and the very small one-year-old daughter who does not yet know about much has been picked up off the dirt floor at the back of the stall and held up closely to your light-skinned face. Very close: and the small one-year-old does not like where she has been brought and does not like the white skin and begins to cry out loudly and to kick and swing her small bare legs and arms wildly in the air. And the crowd is now laughing even more loudly and the madam is continuing to smile broadly at you and to bargain with you over the price of the treasured tins of margarine; and the oldest daughters with the high cheekbones and the olive-smooth black skin are also smiling broadly, and laughing, and seemingly embarrassed when they see you looking at them as they quietly and busily arrange the large stacks of canned foods on display on the tables at the back of the stall in the shade of the shed roofs. But sometimes the smiling leaves them and they will stop and look up deeply into your eyes. And the crowd is continuing to grow around the stall and now the very old uncle who sits for most of the day at the back in the shade and watches the stall when the madam leaves is also brought up to the front by a daughter to look, and when he comes into the light you see why he has to sit all day because of the bad leg that is covered with the white and pinkish disease and that no longer works. And you try not to look straight at it and so only see the thick swarm of flies out of the corner of your eye and then quickly it is time to think of the wide ocean and the strong wind blowing spray off the tops of the slow-rolling swells. But the bone-arm of the old skin-and-bones uncle does work, and so does the laugh, and, raising his bone-arm up at you and extending a long, pointing finger, he grins widely and out of the yellowish mouth that still has several teeth comes a high, whining laugh; and you want to look at him and laugh back but have to look away when the accompanying spittle becomes dark.

And then out comes the oldest daughter with the very smooth black-olive skin, and it is the deepest of blacks and the most pleasantly smooth of skins and the high pronounced cheekbones are very wide and the eyes very wide and dark; and she also has come out from the crowd of people sitting on the low benches in the shade near the back and all the young men around the stall now come quickly forward and point at the lovely, smooth-skinned girl. And the oldest brother has come the farthest forward and asks in English that you take his smooth-skinned sister who is now trying to cover her loud laughter with her hands and who never looks at your face as she moves back behind the food-stacked rows of tables. She is probably married and with several small children, but she is yours to take for a wife. She will make you very strong babies, the older brother is telling you loudly in English, and you will both like the babies very much; and the very heavy and perspiring madam behind the main table and the old uncle leaning against a post of the high overhead roof, and all the young men and the younger daughters in the crowd surrounding you at the stall are moving closer to encourage you to consider their very beautiful sister. You have come for margarine, but a daughter is being offered; and they are all coming up closer and laughing louder and the embarrassed but still laughing daughter has now gone to hide completely behind the tall stack of bags of coco-yams at the back of the stall. And you are hoping that they are not serious but you know they are and that they would quickly and gladly send a daughter off with you even before they knew your name and that she would truly want to go. But she is something to look at; and you remember the restless evenings at your small African house in the bush. And she is very feminine, but you also sense, strongly, her great pride and inner strength. And the dark skin is so very smooth, and, with the short dress, you notice greatly the strong smooth body. But it is becoming later in the day and you have to finish up in Accra and so try to think of what there is still left to do; but instead you look again at the now quiet woman. And now you are trying not to think at all: thinking is killing you; but how can you not think of what might be going on this very minute at home, 9,000 miles away, with her, where it is night, and he is probably enjoying himself; a lot. The bastard. So you pay the still-laughing madam for the margarine and put the two large cans into your cloth shoulder bag; and the nearest small children reach out quickly to touch your arm and feel the fine hairs once more before you leave, and call out more loudly and boldly to you; and the old uncle laughs his whining grin-laugh. And the beautiful older daughter has stopped smiling and is now looking wide-eyed and straight at you; and, saying good bye loudly in the local dialect to the crowd at the stall, and waving good bye, you turn and move back into the packed market corridor as the stall-crowd calls out loudly thanking you, and laughing, and calling good bye; and after only a short distance down the crowded narrow lane you are out of their sight except for the two small brothers who have followed you for several stalls.

And it is hot in there, and loud, and there is a lot of garbage, and they try to take care of it; but there are buzzards on the piles, though. Right in hot Makola Market, a lot of garbage from the spoiled food that is thrown out, and the unused stalks and skins that are thrown onto the ground from the selling tables, and around the butcher-block houses the bones and some unused meat; and there are workers who are paid to get the garbage into piles and all throughout there are large open areas where the garbage is supposed to go, but that is the problem: it is all throughout. And the very large buzzards with the drooping pink necks and the long hooking beaks, and the large black eyes, stay very near to the garbage; boy, do they ever stay near it. Like right on it, and a lot of them, and they don't seem to mind much. They are embarrassing, too, because they don't seem to care what people think about them being on the large piles, and they are very tall and you can't help but not like them for that and for coming right down into friendly local Makola; and you try to look at them angrily but they just look back and then you have to look away because it is too difficult to look at a nearby bird that does not give into your staring and lets you know it. And you know they don't care that you see them walking about the garbage, and that you wish they would leave it alone and act afraid like they should, or at least be sneaky and not be so big. And they are very tall birds but not like any bird that you have ever seen before, and so you have to look away because the more they see you getting angry the happier they become and the more they will bend down to dig. But they are also very large and do not look like they could move very fast so why would they get so close to where people are? If you walk too closely they will just leap over a ways, but, actually, you are trying not to look at them at all because you are trying not to breathe in that area. It is hard enough breathing in the hot crowds of Makola away from the garbage areas, but in them, with the tall buzzard-birds walking and eating about the high piles and many others perched on the tops of the surrounding shed roofs, and a few more circling slowly in the air high above; and, surely, by the grace-of-God, surely, one or two large Makola sewers in the area, there you are trying not to breathe at all because exactly what do you think it is that you are breathing? Air? I don't think so, but I guess it would have to be; but it is so very hot and your clothing is soaked through with sweat from the heat and humidity and you have to wonder a lot about what the *juju* you are doing in such a place; but you get very worrisome when you breathe in. Yes, you can easily begin to think that this is not a place where you had thought you would have wanted to be, especially after college, that it is not what you thought you had meant by the future, and that if she had had any doubts before she wouldn't have any now if she could see where it is you have brought yourself to, on your own; because walking through the open airless-area in the hot African sun you can't help but be having doubts, and could understand her probably being glad you were away, and wanting to be with someone else: someone who would not go to where there was no air to breathe. Although in the recent last letter she had said how very much she missed you, and so awaited your return, and how her love for you was truly great; but, still, you would not resist her going to someone else and in fact would probably encourage it, because it is clear now that it would be a great waste of time trying to make something of someone who would come here to this place. But it is your own fault and you can't figure out why you ever left that job back home that you hated with the wrath of the Devil—*ha, ha*—and the very pleasant city neighborhoods with the small coffee-houses and bookstores and the people like yourself, all for this place, without her; but you are not really alone with the tall buzzard standing uncaringly up ahead on the large fly-covered Makola food pile and the hot sun beating down strongly high above. And the thing seems to have found something to be eating that it can lift up off the pile just as you come unbreathingly past; and it does not care that you do not like it and knows that you don't know what to do about a bird that is as large as an animal and that thinks it's humorous for being so unbird-like and for spending most of its day in the private garbage area of your fellow humans; and trying not to look for too long at the bird and the part that is hanging down from the beak, you want badly to kick the tall bird-animal for probably having caused the woman to have left, you think.

But, really, anyway, you do have areo-grams, and now margarine, and that is something to have in West Africa; but it is just that there are times when it gets very frustrating because you want to do the night things and can't stop thinking about it. And Makola Market will do these things to you: cause your mind to wonder off and make you keep thinking human; but if it is happening a lot it may be that the charms are nearby and that can make your skin crawl if you think about it. But, I know: you don't believe in the charms, in that sort of thing, you don't believe in the African black-magic. Then why does it cause so many things to happen and for you to lose your very fine American girl friend who is 7,000 miles away in a pleasant bookstore and get the local black buzzards thinking a lot about you; and this will only go on when you are probably very near to one of the old fetish stalls with the many small piles of fine powders spread out on the mats on the stall floors and the old, smiling, bearded *Wulomei* sitting alone in the shadows on a stool beyond the mats; I think: unless the stalls are not in the area after all but back across the market somewhere on the other side. But you are sure that there is one nearby so how else can you explain it? But sometimes you've just got to get of Makola, you've got to get out of there. There are times when during the heat and thick crowds of the mid-afternoon that that is the best thing to do, and you know it is, and so can only hope that the buzzard-birds don't try to stop and question you too much about leaving and that the crowd will not try too hard to touch your extremely humorous skin or laugh too loudly at the sight of your God-forsaken face.

So moving once again in the afternoon heat through the crowded narrow inner-Makola corridors, you make your way out of the market and back to the car-and-people-packed street running alongside the vehicle-jammed central lorry station, and, feeling hungry and needing to sit again and be away from the crowds and out of the mid-afternoon sun, you decide to make your way to Kinbu Street on the other side of the blocks-long lorry station to find the small *Fauzi's* Lebanese restaurant with the cheap hot food and the cold bottles of *Star* beer. *Star* beer? What is *Star* beer. It is only the very finest brewed beer in all of West Africa; unless you have traveled to Bamako in the interior and can find the precious bottles of *Premium*. But *Star* is no ordinary beer because, you see, there are some very interesting things about it. Such as *Heineken*. Does the name *Heineken* ring any bells? It should, because it is an excellent beer and well known, and, well, it was the *Heineken* company that built the *Star* brewery in Accra during the great second-world-war that our mighty fathers fought boldly to the bloody death. But to blessed hell with the souls of our forefathers who brought the alive West Africans to fight in that God-cursed white-man's war. —From here? Took there? To fight and die? I could not have fought; I could not have taken the blood. But it was long before my time so what does it matter now in very hot Accra with the tall, green palms bending back from the edge of the sea and the glistening white igloos lining the beach. ...I said igloos lining the beach. ...Igloos? Ha! I am only kidding. I am only making sure that you are paying attention to what it is that I am telling about and that is this: that war is a bad thing; a very bad thing. It is the god-given truth and I am not lying about it so stop doubting me all the time. Besides, what do you know? Anything? I doubt it. I doubt it as a bloody buzzard walks a high pile. But we all know some things; there are just some things that we all know about; all of us. You've got to believe me and try to start feeling good again. We can be friends but you've got to understand to try at it. Anyway, the *Fantis'* along the coast toward Takoradi will be your friends, I'm telling you they will.

But having gone through Makola can leave you dead tired, but also very thrilled, because there is just an awful lot going on in Makola: a lot that you had never realized before or could even have tried to think about because the way things are in Makola is so very different from how you had been told they are. And although you know that you can only take going into Accra and the central market every now and then, you never stop thinking about it, or about being around some of the very unusual things that go on there. It may, though, have something to do with the heat.

But you should try to get to the *Fauzi's* food place so that you can rest before you try to get anymore done today in prosperous Accra. ...Hello? Did you catch that one? Prosperous Accra! Ha! Do you really think it's prosperous around here? Let me put it to you this way and then you can think about it; a lot if you'd like: How can an entire city that when you walk into any one of the many large government food stores you see nothing but rows and rows of empty shelves be called prosperous? It can't, so I won't call it the mighty word prosperous anymore; no, I'll choose a different word. Like: poor. I'm afraid that that is the best word to use to describe a place where, because the government has stolen much of the national profits and badly mismanaged the once rich economy, you now see nothing but row after row of empty shelves in every store in the country. And there are not even the basic commodities of soap or cooking oil or kerosene. But don't think for even a minute that the pride of the people of this place is anything but strong, or that they have anything less than the richest of souls, or are anything but strongest of strong in spirit, because to believe anything else would be very far from the truth. They have lived proudly in the area for many hundreds of years and are not going to fall over and die because the Western man's fragrant soap cannot be found in any store or merchants stall in the country. No, they are very alive with the strengths of their ways, and their spirits are strong; even though the great slave trade cut cleanly through their souls and wrought much havoc on the once strong structures of the people and set up what became the conquering and exploitation by the great seafaring Europeans; and the tall, white-walled castles that stored first the gold and then the captives who were brought in from the interior, still line the coast; and when you go down the dark sloping stone-tunnels that connect the lower levels of the castles to where the skiffs floated up to the seaward walls to transport the cargo out to the waiting ships in the harbor, you can still see the chains on the walls where they were kept until the skiff came because they have now strung up electric lights along the dark corridor walls; and there is also some light coming in from the tunnel's seaward end where the surf crashes up onto the rocks just out the opening.

But you have got to get out of the crowd and sit and rest, and, so, continuing along Boham street beside the vehicle-packed lorry station in the midday heat, you make your way through the crowd to smaller Obwasi Street. And moving up Obwasi and seeing the small *Fauzi's* sign beside the open door leading into the long narrow eating place wedged between the modern hardware business on one side and the older appliance business on the other at the street level of the old two-story cement building, you enter out of the bright sunlight into the dimly lit restaurant with the overhead ceiling fans and the small cloth-covered tables with the few local businessmen drinking beer, and sit at one of the tables and look at one of the small worn, single-page menus. And the light-skinned Lebanese waiter comes to your table and takes your order for the days hot meat-stew with rice, and a bottle of beer; but you may be by yourself and if so you may wonder about having one of the strong beers alone; but you have done it enough times before in crowded Accra and they serve the smaller bottles at *Fauzi's* and it is hot, and, besides, what other pleasures are there is life? So the bottle comes and it is pleasant inside out of the sun and crowd, and, looking back across the dim narrow restaurant, you see the bright sunlight outside through the open door, and, briefly, the crowd and traffic moving by in the street. And it feels good to be sitting in a quiet place after the central market; but you have been brought back to life and learned much from Makola, and, drinking the beer, you remember the excitement of the crowd and how funny the birds had seemed.

But it is getting late to try to get much more done this day in Accra; and there is plenty more to have tried to do: forms for the plane tickets to Tanzania and visa stamps for Togo (but that is back across all of Accra to where the rows of embassies sit amongst the large, old British colonial homes) or checking the savings account at *Standard Bank* back by Parliament House or going to read the American magazines at the U.S. Information Agency; but what you really think about are the carving shops back toward Ring Road that, once, fifteen years before, were jammed full with excellent old *Mossi* and *Bambara* carvings and the tiny bronze *Ashanti* figurines. And the shops once did a thriving business but now mostly have fake tourist pieces; but in the backs of the stores on the higher shelves there are still some larger older pieces that would be worth having the shop keeper bring down. But it is getting late and finally your plate of steaming hot food comes and after drinking down more of the beer and still feeling good about where you are and what you have accomplished, you begin to eat the spicy food, but this causes you to begin thinking human again. But, no, you try not to think: and so imagine the room back home that will house the fine African wood-figures that you know you can find if you just look hard enough.

But you must decide what you should try to do for the rest of the hot afternoon in Accra, what it is you should try to get done. Although sometimes you can't really get anything done in an entire day in Accra and then it is just having gone out into the crowds that will have made it all worthwhile, because to have even left the rest house compound and gone out by yourself into the alive Accra crowd is not a small thing.

And finishing the rice stew and the bottle of beer, and remembering how later, someday, you would be glad if you had one of the good carvings, you decide to head out toward Ring Road where you once remember having seen several of the older carving stores from within a crowded bus on an earlier trip into the city. So you finish the last of the bottle and now do not care about the people who will be pointing and laughing, and, paying at the counter for the meal and beer, go back out into the bright sunlight and the crowd and begin the long hot walk through the city to Kente Street near National Liberation Circle and the few, old, nearly-deserted carving shops at the street level of some of the small cement buildings of the area. And moving away from the central trading district the street becomes less clogged and the crowds on the broken sidewalks and dirt beside the street begin to thin out; and small cement houses begin appearing between the lower, humidity-stained buildings of the area. And taking palm-tree-lined back-streets back to crowded and traffic-clogged Liberty Avenue, you move steadily in the heat up the wide busy street with the tall, cement, modern-art piece of *Liberation Circle* faintly visible through the haze in the far distance at an outer edge of the city. And reaching, finally, a two-story cement building housing one of the carving and tribal-cloth businesses, you enter into the carving-packed front room where sitting on a low wood stool behind a glass cabinet filled with tiny brass figurines and cheap leather crafts is the clerk who smiles gently as you come in. And in the back there are some older looking pieces and some quite large that are up high and you see now some of the tall old *Mossi* antelope-masks, each with the long extending chin section curving down four feet from the painted wood face, and the flat, shorter horn-like extension protruding up from the top of the forehead.

Yes, these are different you see. Finer pieces that were left over or missed by the swarms of earlier art hunters. And reaching up and bringing the tall white-and-dark-red-checked mask down from the wall, you look closely at the aging paint and try to decide how old the piece is; but mostly you just decide about it from how it looks to you, and the feeling that it gives, and if you feel that there is anything special about it.

But the old *Mossi* mask in the back of the deserted carving store is too big to try to take back now; unless you are on your way out of the country and can take it directly to the airport for shipping; but with the size of the box that you would need you would want to include other items. So you look instead at the many smaller carvings hoping to find one of the hatchet-faced *Dogon* figures with the long bending knees and pointed breasts. But there are only the small, female *Ewe'* heads, carved from low-grade ebony; but sometimes you come across one with a special face that was made by a special carver; and it is of heavy black ebony and the female's fine face is such that you sense it is giving off something special, and you will want to look at the carving again in another place and know that it will again give off the same feeling, and it is a peaceful feeling that is not a lot unlike the sight of the cresting swells approaching the shore on the wide, wind-swept ocean.

But the quiet older store clerk wants fifty cedis for the carving, and even if you could get him down to twenty-five you still would not have enough left to eat at a good restaurant this evening which, after many months in the bush, you had promised yourself you would do. And now that you have seen that there are some older carvings in the shop, and you know that rarely does anyone come into the store anymore; not since the local economy deteriorated five years before and the carving hunters and tourists stopped coming—except for the few, young, money-less travelers from Europe and Australia and North America who still make the difficult journey into the harsh region—so knowing this, that you can come back later and buy what you want, you begin to think about ending the day in Accra and of eventually making your way back to the rest house and what it will take to do that: walking in the late-afternoon heat back to the crowded commercial area and finding a taxi to take you back out Cantoments Road.

So smiling goodbye to the quiet clerk you do that: leave the deserted carving store and go back out into the noisy street and begin the long walk back up Liberty Avenue where, in the distance, the higher buildings of the commercial district surrounding Makola Market are faintly visible rising into the hazy air. And moving up the broken cement sidewalk beside the deep sewer running alongside the traffic-clogged street, there is more calling out from the small children as the crowd gradually thickens, but because you are now tired and still feeling some of the effects of the beer you do not notice them so much, or care that they are causing the crowd to stop and look at you coming up the sidewalk. And then comes the heavy traffic of inner Accra and the hazy blue smoke high in the air above the city from the exhausts and the burning of garbage and the thousands of small cooking fires.

And it is becoming much later in the afternoon and you have been walking since you left the rest house early this morning and are beginning to think a lot now about the quiet, old, rest house sitting-room with the many comfortable chairs and the bookcase filled with the many fine books left behind by earlier travelers.

But you are also feeling good from just having come into Accra, and from what you have gotten done, and the business part of the day is ending and so you decide to go to the food and beer bar on the outdoor balcony above the Post Office with the pleasant view looking down onto the busy street below and out over an edge of the market, and, there, sit and drink a glass of the cheaper *Red Knight* beer before trying to get a taxi back to the rest house.

And coming back into the thickest of crowded Accra and moving back along Selwyn Street bordering the market and then past the tall G.N.T.C. building in the core of the commercial area before coming again, for the second time today, to the smaller Post Office building, you climb the outside steps up to the noisy bar on the second-story balcony that wraps around the outside of the old cement building where, sitting at small tables spread about the balcony, many small groups of local people are bent over glasses of beer, and talking loudly and laughing, and seemingly drunk; but a lot of that is just what happens to you from the heat and humidity and the crowdedness of Accra.

And although there are many people and it is loud with end-of-the-day drinkers, there are still plenty of empty tables, and, getting your beer from the server and going to one of the tables at the edge of the cement balcony, you sit in one of the small folding chairs and look out over the smoky market and the crowded street below.

And leaning back in the chair and taking the weight off your dirty sandaled-feet, you now feel the soreness of your legs from the many long miles you have walked today in Accra, and, while sipping steadily from the large glass of cool beer, the aching slowly leave your body. And taking in the alive colorful setting below, you see now that the movement of people at the visible edge of the market is slower, and fewer, and mostly outward; and everywhere large, cloth-wrapped bundles and baskets of goods balanced on people's heads are being moved out for storage for the night.

And drinking long again from the beer and watching the crowd below, you feel relaxed and content and pleased with how you have spent the day and with what you have accomplished although eventually the large carvings will be difficult to ship and she and her friends and your friends may not think that much about them later.

But, still, the view is good and the beer very relaxing and looking further now into the distance, the edge of the ocean can be seen, and, vaguely, the tall white-stone-walls of the Presidential Castle, eastward along the distant shore.

So with the sun now beginning to go down fast and a few lights about the city coming on, you drink down more of the beer and think of how out in the bush the heat is really not so bad as long as you can stay out of the sun for most of the day, which just means that you have to spend the day in your room. But you can always read then, and write, and reread the letters that she has so dutifully sent over the months and that have helped you not to worry so. Everything is fine, no doubt; she will still love you dearly when you do finely return, even though you cannot expect her to wait forever. If there is someone else now, though, you will just go to see her and hope that it is not going well with him then. But you also know that she will not be able to wait much longer and soon you must decide about staying or going back, or going somewhere else. Another year, though, might be too long to be away; but then you for sure could get to Bobo Dioulasso to the north and there find the finest carvings in all of West Africa. But another year would make it two years away and you do not know if she could wait that long. You, though, could easily wait that long because it would just mean delaying making a commitment which is something at which you are a true specialist. You have delayed and avoided them all your life, and then desperately avoided the great fear that someday you will have to pay for all the avoiding. But you try, honestly, and with all your great inner strength which you derived from growing up in a split-level housing-tract in Toledo, Ohio, or Santa Barbara, California, or Beaverton, Oregon, in the 1950s and 60s, to make just one small commitment to anything, but it never works. You have always had too great an attraction to excitement, and the possibility of excitement, and you don't want anyone else having more excitement than yourself. And you have become so good at finding excitement everywhere and in everything, that you have even learned the great art of disguising excitement as some kind of commitment. Look at me, you say, I am a truly responsible person: look at this difficult commitment I have made; but really there is a great new thrill nearby that you are planning to sneak in. They have always thought you were sneaky and have never trusted you, but it is because they are jealous. And you cannot stop it, even though at a great personal expense you have tried. Well, she will just have to wait, they will all have to wait, you will have to wait. And pray that it does not become too late.

And drinking down the remainder of the beer, you decide that you will remain in the region for the time being and continue to make the pleasant trips into Accra. And now beginning another beer, and looking out over the darkening city, you feel that everything will be fine with her and that even a month in Egypt will have to be made before you finally do return for good. You probably will not be on an adventure like this again and so should see and do all that you can. Anyway, it would only mean another few months away, unless there is more to see there than Pete had talked about. It was a very exciting place, he had said.

Hmmmmm.

On the Wide African Plain

"All right!" the woman yelled from the front seat of the car, her window half down, which she quickly rolled up as the man, who had been out the driver's door, shot back in and slammed the door shut. The lions, which had been resting near a bush and leaped to their feet the moment Mark had grabbed for the branch, now stood motionless, glancing to the side, panting in the hot afternoon sun, only at times looking directly at them. In the distance, rising up from the vast plain, the snow-capped summit of Mt. Kilimanjaro floated in the cloudless sky.

Alice looked at the mountain which gave her some peace because she could relive the excitement of the climb: the non-stop fun, if you were in shape like she was, an experienced Sierra-Club guide; the invincibility of youth; the surprisingly quick letting-go to Mark (although she had not been all that impressed at first); the future very promising, especially for what might be in store when they got back down to the base lodge and the group split up.

But the peace left the moment she turned and saw the lions again who had now been there for two days, who had almost gotten her when they had first become stuck in the sandy creek bed, trying to take a short-cut, and been out with river debris attempting to dig out the tires. Then one of the big females had come crouching toward them and leaped the instant Alice had seen her and screamed, and just managed to dive into the backseat as the claws of the swiping front leg caught her shirt and waist. They had both screamed then; they hadn't seen a lion in three days of dawn to dusk searching; bad luck, they thought, they'd seen every other big and small game the Amboselli Reserve had to offer. But then they had been so preoccupied with freeing the car, so close to getting it out: it had felt like just another Midwest January-day in a snow bank; inconvenient, but typically dumb to have gotten stuck; now just get the damn thing out. But the primordial shock of being leaped at by a physically superior carnivore changed them, forever (in a way that standing on the summit of Kilimanjaro, on the roof of Africa, never could) and then the whole pride attacking, leaping onto the hood, rising on hind legs to claw at the still partially opened windows which they frantically rolled up, and then instinctively locked the doors as though it were a mugger, as they both screamed again and soiled their pants.

"That's it—that's it."

Mark breathed heavily, the adrenaline still streaming through his veins: there would be no more trying to jam sticks under the tires, at least until it again seemed like the only good plan. He leaned on the horn, blasting its city trumpet in the heart of the East African savanna, annoying but not frightening the King of the Jungle, mostly in the faint hope that another vehicle might happen to be above the gully, with windows lowered enough to hear a horn from an unseen automobile.

They had run out of non-rescue things to say to each other by the middle of the first morning. These two strangers; fools for love, attempting to quench the sex drive that the King of the Jungle now periodically flaunted in the nearby grass with his in-heat mate: the big male, his thick mane glistening in the sun, mounting and humping. Sort of like they had done at the cheap one-star Nyeri Hotel in Nairobi for three days after the climb. Eight celibate days on an African trek would do that to you, or to them; the two single ones with the lowest amount of willpower and sense of self-worth. Eight days with a married quarreling, American-couple; an enviable living together British-couple; and two older men in long term marriages whom it seemed would at least have the option of humping, hopefully, every now and then.

But not Alice and Mark. Experienced: yes; but able to make serious commitments: no. They were too liberated. From what they weren't sure: something, though, that they had both spent a great deal of time and energy creating in their minds: Fucking gets old after a while. Why not keep it fresh; vibrant; messy.

There wasn't much more to say; denial, deeply entrenched, was in no hurry to leave: this wasn't really happening was it? Like some cheap 'B' movie. The car was stuck in a dry riverbed, down a gully and hidden from sight, miles and miles into the open expanse of the Amboselli Reserve. The return flights to the States were separate affairs: the earliest, Mark's, was not scheduled for six more days; Alice had planned to roam for three months; she had said something about Egypt. No one was expecting them back anytime soon, so no one was likely to report them missing for weeks, at the earliest.

"I still can't believe we haven't seen anyone on the other side," Mark said, his voice drained and tired, having not spoken of that particular rescue fantasy since morning; and he looked beyond the opposite bank to where there was at least some visible distance of land, unlike behind them where a bend in the river had eroded a twelve foot cliff that would obscure whatever was below. But they had left the main dirt track a quarter of a mile from there anyway, so unless someone else had the same bad idea they had, of taking the obscure minor track east, to cross the riverbed and pick up the highway at the base of the

Mau escarpment—where they knew the highway was—no one was going to be coming.

"No game...no game..." Alice said forlornly, and reached over and pulled him toward her; and he leaned into her shoulder and breast, the dried blood from the flesh wound still discoloring her shirt, their shit-filled underwear having long before been thrown out the window and dragged away by wild dogs. Carloads of tourists crisscrossed the plain looking for game. See a few cars in the distance and know they had found something. That's where all the vehicles were.

"No game," she said again, "—except them." Neither of them looked. "Shoot, where's Benji when we need him?" Now she smiled and looked again at the mountain; Benji, the Kenyan porter, fresh in both their minds. Befriending all. Bringing an endless and contagious spell of genuine enthusiasm and excitement to the sometimes grueling climb. An authentic local African: *Arusha*; plant cultivator; grade school dropout; sometime cattle-herder, blood-drinker and *Masai* confidant.

"He probably returned to his village. Probably to his wife and kids," Mark said, thinking of the crumpled photos of the two beaming children that had been pulled often from Benji's wallet and displayed to the 'awwwing' foreigners. "Probably resting comfortably in his home."

*   *   *

The aging Datsun pickup came to a dusty stop at the side of the empty road and the African near the rear leaped to the ground with his bag. "Olesérè—olesérè—a-serían e-lótótó. " *Maa-Irusa* goodbyes were exchanged with the driver and several other passengers and the pickup left in another cloud of dust as the African headed on foot through the short scrub across the plain toward the cluster of mud and cement houses in the distance.

When he reached his home in the center of the village amidst the wandering goats and chickens, and the running children, and entered the compound, his two girls ran out to him, as his wife, with the baby wrapped tight to her back in the bright *Ajiara* cloth, pounded the wood mortar with the maize pestle under the tin shelter of the outdoor kitchen. Benji's wife, gripping the four-foot pestle with both hands, pounding, greeted him in their native *Irusa* and told him another telegram had come from Mombasa and that it was on the front table. She told him that immediately because she knew that would be what he would most want to know about; even before knowing that the maize crop had grown so big in the month he had been away climbing Rick mountain that they would be bringing in maybe two-hundred schillings more than last year. But she knew he would want to know first about his sister.

*   *   *

The tire was deep, spinning, going nowhere; a pathetic little Toyota Corolla, the cheapest rental they could find. The lions had suddenly gotten up and left; something of greater interest had come to their attention. After an hour, slowly—really, in slow-motion—with Alice closely scouting the terrain, Mark had opened the door, gotten out, and jammed one more branch under the tire.

The tire quickly spun the branch out from underneath.

"Shit, well, we weren't going to be doing any of this off road crap," Mark said disgustedly as he shut off the engine, remembering the more expensive Range Rover they had declined. "—I knew we shouldn't have come down here."

"Oh, fuck you," Alice said in disbelief and leaned away. "You were the one who kept talking about cutting over to the highway."

"Yeah, but not down here. I thought we—"

"Mark...they're back..." They were back; one of the big females dragging the body of a gazelle to the same bush they had been under before. "Christ, this is probably their den, their home—look, over there, are those bones!" Alice spoke incredulously and rolled her window up to a more reassuring height. "They probably smell our food."

"They smell us," Mark said.

"They smell our fear; honest to god—I read that once, lions can actually smell fear."

Mark blew the horn again and turned up the static from the radio as high as it would go, neither of which elicited even a look.

"Mark—we should save the battery."

He stopped and gripped the wheel, staring into the brown expanse, and slowly lowered into the seat. "...Are you thirsty?"

"Yes—I'm parched," Alice said. "We're going to have to get water. Somehow, someway."

"Where, Alice, there isn't any?"

She sat silently for a moment in the car seat, looking up again at Kilimanjaro with its glistening snow-cap. "There was sure a lot on the mountain....remember the falls?"

"Well, I remember you," Mark said, and he pulled her back toward him.

They had stopped at the second camp in a deep valley beside a stream in the late afternoon, and people had gone to a pool below a small waterfall to cool off and wash for the last time before the next day's climb to the final base-camp below the summit. The experienced group of climbers now bonded and randy enough after five days together for the girls to strip to athletic bras and underwear to soak in the shallow water. Pumped and perpetually horny Mark getting his first complete view of a dripping Alice emerging from the cool water, a view he had been trying to accurately formulate for days through various layers of mountaineering clothing. Having to force himself to look away, out to the enormous expanse below, away from a sight which now seemed tormenting: a wet, dripping, half-naked Alice. Chirpy, flirty, Alice; curvy, very curvy; and then slender; and then—good Jesus—curves that caused the quickening of his pulse. Mark had had to sit down on the spongy grass as she quickly wrapped a towel around her lower half and dabbed at the moisture that clung to her skin.

I'll never forget you that first time at the stream," he said in the car on the barren plain. "God, with the sun shining down...it was torture, pure torture."

Alice grinned. "Yeah, well...I was hot... And we hadn't bathed in a couple of days." She smiled again knowing that was only half the story. The Utah boys back home where she lived always lacking in some way, shape, or form. Especially up at the ski lodge where she worked during the winters, never quite making the cut. Older men from somewhere else with their sad, awkward passes, or local kids with their boorish slurs to the tall Amazonian living amongst them. Who knows who you'll meet on a *Mountain Mania* expedition, the same company that had introduced her to Craig in Patagonia two years before—even though he did have a wife and kids; but it was still fun. Well, people who are inspired to travel to Africa, anyway; not like Tom, the *Park City* lift-operator, her on and off-again boyfriend—or so he thought. And there's always more men than women on these foreign expeditions, so at least the odds are favorable.

What luck, Mark thought, at having run into Alice; there's usually not that many women on these foreign climbs. But he had hoped there might be a few; at least they would have world-trekking in common. Not like the women back home in that backwater Missouri town where he had accidentally ended up pursuing his municipal planning career, who seemed seldom even to get out of the local county. He looked at the water container on the car floor that was down to two inches and would be gone by tomorrow. They had used too much cleaning Alice's wound, he thought; he had tried not to show his dissonance as he had tried to be the protective, sacrificing male. Sacrificing for his mate. His mate? They had known each other for two weeks. They just knew how to fornicate like mates.

Alice looked down at the cloth that covered her wound. It had not been deep, but was still red and sore; the outfitters had warned about the dangers of infections in Africa. She wished she could have cleaned it better but could tell Mark was worrying about using too much water. Big deal, she thought. In this heat, sooner or later, when they ran out, and the lions left again, one or both of them was going to have to try and make it to the highway.

"Listen..." Mark said suddenly.

"Yeah—there." Alice pointed to the far horizon and the source of the low drone. Like a mechanical insect, the speck of a small plane moved low across the sky.

"*Come on,*" Mark said anxiously, trying to coax it toward them. But it continued angling away and then was gone. "—We need to build a fire. We need to do something."

Fifty feet away in the shade of the river brush, in a half circle that faced the car, the lions worked on the gazelle.

*　　　*　　　*

On the aging platform of the Nairobi train station, at the far end of the Mombasa line—four-hundred miles and fourteen hours from the Indian Ocean—in the heat and chaos of the platform crowd, Benjamin Kiyati, with his travel bag over his shoulder and a tightly clutched ticket in his hand, pushed toward the open door in the crush of passengers boarding the third-class coach as the sun descended on the distant hills and turned the thick smog and smoke of Nairobi crimson and orange.

With the pleading voices of the weak echoing in between the defiant shouts of the strong, he squeezed through the door and into the aisle as a conductor, pushing, grabbing, threatening, pulled into the car the last possible body before sliding shut the door. A moment later, with an initial lurch that sent the unprepared sprawling, the train moved forward, slow chug after slow chug, the crowd inside louder than ever, jockeying for space that did not exist, the seats long before packed and overflowing. Out the half-opened windows, the smoke-filled shacks of the train-yard shantytown passed slowly by as a yelling mob ran temporarily alongside in the dirt.

*   *   *

Richard Boyle, Nebraska native and university graduate, Vietnam veteran, husband and father, chief State Department criminal investigator for East Africa stationed at the American embassy in Nairobi, set the *Nairobi Standard* he had been reading onto his lap and watched the last of the ramshackle shantytowns of the outskirts of Nairobi pass by the window of the four-person couchette compartment of the Mombasa sleeper. Now the train picked up speed, clanking loudly down the iron tracks and out onto the plain, the last of the city disappearing and the sweeping grasslands of East Africa spreading into the horizon like a great rolling sea, catching the last rays of the setting sun which lowered into the Rift Valley behind. The three other passengers, with whom he had casually spoken upon their initial seating, now all gazed silently out the window at the passing plain. Approaching in the near distance, below a tall stand of outward-spreading acacias, the elongated necks and sloping bodies of two giraffes moved slowly through the deep grass, their brown and white-patched hides catching the sun's last rays.

Just beyond, in a grassless swath of barren earth, a small herd of zebras stood motionless in the fading light.

As the train sped to the east and darkness descended, Richard Boyle, now seeing more of the reflected, electrically-lit compartment out the window than the Kenyan landscape—particularily, just inches away, his own aging face—again raised the *Nairobi Standard* from his lap, as slowly did the others in the compartment, with the various books and periodicals they held in their hands.

*   *   *

"Look—the mountain." Alice pointed up to where Kilimanjaro had just reappeared from behind the clouds that engulfed most of the summit.

"It's got to rain around here sometime," Mark said. "Benji kept talking about the rains coming, like this was some big deal, remember?"

"Oh yeah, he sounded like a forecaster: *'lope-a-row'*, or whatever he called it. Some special storm. Like it only came every ten years or something."

"Yeah, that was the only thing that seemed to bother him for the whole climb—wanting to get down before *'bad lope-a-row'*. Peter seemed sort of concerned too. Well, they kept discussing it anyway." Now the summit was gone again and the clouds swept low toward the plain.

"Don't you think Judy and Tim bothered Benji,

too?" Alice said. "They sure bothered everyone else. Especially Peter."

Judy and Tim, the young American couple from San Fransico, alternating between blissful love and brutal contempt. One fight culminating in a serious attempt by Judy to have Peter, the head guide who shared a tent with Linda, his assistant, swap tents for the night so Judy would not have to sleep with Tim. Under no circumstances was this going to happen under Peter's watch, and only after Benji and Linda spoke with them were they persuaded to make up and alleviate any fears of what may have happened if Tim had been forced outside for a night in the cold mountain air. Of course Alice and Mark, and the other six members, mostly found this hilarious and entertaining, as the spectacular scenery and shear thrill of the climb could hardly be dampened by a pair of feuding lovers.

"Yeah, for a while there I think Peter wasn't going to let them summit," Mark said.

Alice looked again toward the mountain, part of which was now coming back into view as the clouds parted to one side. "What a place..." she said dreamily, remembering the summit where the cracking blocks of towering glaciers surrounded them like the abandoned buildings of a city street.

They had arisen from the tin hiking-huts of Kibo camp in total darkness and with headlamps ascended the final four-thousand vertical-feet to the summit. The occasional speckled lights of distant towns visible on the plain below, arriving just as the rays of the morning sun bathed the summit from the far, eastern horizon. They huddled together on a west facing slope, heavily bundled from head to toe, the wind howling and unavoidable, mesmerized by the enormous distance of vision, sipping from water bottles, eating power-bars, and snapping photos of each other and the great expanse below.

On the heat of the plain, beside the river brush, the lions, not in a sharing mood, growled as they tore at the gazelle.

*   *   *

"...These Swahili, they will scrape and scrape at your spirit, like jackels; the sailors, they have made them mighty, like ants making dirt into a fort...what good is dirt?"

Benji, in the packed train car, listened to the *Kikuyu* businessman sitting on the rattling floor beside him. They had been squeezed into their spot by the crowd, now quieter, many sleeping, the screeching metal cylinder speeding across the dark Tsavo expanse, where predators and prey performed their three-act plays between the curtains of sunset and sunrise. The man, Oviyu, who sold advertising to coastal bus lines, had a sister who was married to an *Arusha,* Benji's tribe, and was advising Benji on where best to go in Mombasa and whom best to seek out. For if Benji hoped to save Angie, his sister, he would need all the advice and information he could possibly acquire. And if Kenneth, Angie's boyfriend, had been indebted to a *Swahili* clan, then it was the *Swahili* that Benji would have to appease.

"These foreign sailors," Oviyu went on in *Maa Irusa*, "they have destroyed the port. They bring money and dreams. The girls, they are easily seduced by the Swahili, and then..." he snapped his fingers, "...made to seduce."

Benji leaned his head back and rubbed his eyes. He remembered the fight at home with their parents when Angie had told them she was leaving with Kenneth for Nairobi to work in the hotels. That there was a future there, in the city, where people had lights, and shoes, and pretty clothes. Unlike in Kijiadoi where they would live and die poor, tending the land. But the work had not been there in Nairobi; the violent anti-government demonstrations had begun and the tourists stopped coming. The hotels closed and they lived on the streets until the word spread about Mombasa. That is where the work was now, on the coast, where the port was rapidly expanding for the coming warships. The warships from the other side of the world, with their snapping flags of stars and stripes, that would need a place to stop on their way north to the gulf and the oil fields. There was work in Mombasa.

Oviyu looked at Benji, swaying with the train against the wall. "Ngái is with us," he said. "He is with us all... Here..." He took a small wad of newspaper from his bag and unwrapped a ball of fermented rice and broke off a piece for Benji.

"Thank you...thank you," Benji said to the man, placing a small bit in his mouth and beginning to chew. Now the train began to slow, the loud clanking of the tracks softening and distant lights appearing out the windows. Slower the train rolled, as people began to stir; and a dimly-lit platform appeared and the train came to a stop. Now the lights of the car came on and the talking grew and several people with large bags and overflowing baskets pushed their way to the door and got off. A moment later, an equal number came aboard, their voices at first loud, then quieting as they encountered the packed, half-asleep car.

At the front of the train, from an upper bunk of the couchette compartment, Richard Boyle—sleep having come fitfully—pushed a small corner of the curtain from the window and squinted out at the swarming platform of Voi.

*   *   *

"I know it's over there, three miles at the most. We could be there in an hour." Alice sat low in the passenger seat, perspiring, the windows half down, the afternoon sun striking the car and making heat waves off the hood. The lions panted in the shade of the brush below the bank. To the side lay the gazelle; the swarm of flies hovering like a cloud, visible even from the car. Several large birds ventured up close to the carcass.

Mark looked at the scrub beyond the creek bed. He shook his head. "What if it isn't? What if it's five miles—or ten?"

"Look, you can see the top of the escarpment. If that's more than four miles—I'll...that can't be four miles." A long barren ridge, scarred vertically with dry gullies, crossed the far horizon, like the ridges that were everywhere, in every direction, surrounding the plains and the evaporated lakes and the dry creek beds.

"And what are you going to do when you get there? It could be hours, a day before anyone comes by. We didn't see anyone the last few hours driving to the park. We don't even know if there's a road over there for sure."

Alice squinted in the direction of the ridge.

"The guy at the campground said this track was right after the old airstrip," Mark went on. "Pointed it out right on the map. But it sure seemed like we went a long way before we turned. This might not even be the right road."

"A quarter of a mile, we went a quarter of a mile. You could clearly see it..." Alice's expression now soured. "That prick. *And no problem crossing the creek bed,*" she said sarcastically. "...The guy did it twice in the last week, picked up the highway, zipped up to

Nakura in an hour." Squinting in the glare of the sun, she cleared her throat, then resisted spitting out the window and instead swallowed the saliva. "You know, lions only eat about once a week. They make a kill, they eat, they don't hunt again for days. This might be our chance. That water's going to be gone and we're going to be screwed. No one is ever going to find us down here."

"What are you saying, Alice? You aren't going to try to go to the highway?"

"When they leave—they always go back up the bank—as soon as they're gone, we should go...straight there, no looking back, just like we know what we're doing."

"Alice—you're not serious. ...Look, we can build a fire. Someone's bound to see it. There're planes flying around here all the time."

She gave a contemptuous glance. "One: we've seen one fucking plane in three days. If you didn't notice, that airstrip was abandoned—like from about ten years ago. Two: when the water goes we'll start getting weak, hallucinating, then we'll never make it."

"No...no...I say we stay put. Build a fire. Someone's bound to see it."

Alice looked off. "You do what you want, Mark. I say we head to the highway the first chance we get."

In the shade of the brush, one of the lions rolled onto its back—its thick legs and paws in the air—and twisted in the dirt, then rolled back onto its side and continued panting in the warm afternoon air, as the small dust cloud drifted across the creek bed.

*   *   *

Ann Boyle, dark sunglasses covering her eyes, pulled the Renault out of the Nairobi hospital parking lot and onto the wide, tree-shaded pavement of Kono Boulevard, the buildings of downtown Nairobi rising before her at the bottom of the hill. She drove quickly through the sparse afternoon traffic for the Langata District and Rupert's Toy Store, where she hoped to find something for Maggie, quickly, so she could make it back to the Wilder School in time to pick up Tobin at four. With Richard having been sent back to Mombasa for the investigation, and Maggie's treatments being doubled, there was not enough time to do all that had to be done. It was only with the help of Margaret and Frank, and Alan and Rosanne, who was back at the hospital with Maggie now, and the tight community of employees and their families of the American Mission, that she had been able to survive the nightmare. And Doctor Sanger. Above all, Doctor Sanger. As fine and skilled an oncologist as she had met, and they had met many since the diagnosis. But Nairobi General was also as efficient as one would find anywhere. World class; one legacy of a hundred years of British rule and the deeply-rooted, generations-old British populace.

Little Maggie, too young to really understand, only that she was sick and a lot of nice people really loved her and wanted her to get better; but sometimes what they had to do hurt. Ann had finally come to some peace; she wasn't going to blame God. And she was not going to become bitter and allow the residual of anger to darken whatever light they could muster for their daughter. After the initial shock and anger, there was nothing to be gained from pity. This is how it was and this little creature would know love. Of that there would be no doubt: above all else, she would know love.

To the south there were clouds; it has not rained in weeks, Ann thought, as she pulled onto Uhura Highway. We are due for a good rain, the hills are turning brown again. After this round, if she's strong enough, this weekend we can go to the animal orphanage. She'll be happy to see Doevee, and I think Doevee will be happy to see her.

*   *   *

At eight o'clock in the morning, in the light of the new day, the train passed through the sprawling tropical outskirts of Mombasa and into the city—the occasional green cluster of coconut and palm trees rising in the alleys between the low, white-walled buildings—slowing to a crawl as it entered the humidity-stained station before coming to a stop. From his seat on the floor, Benji stood with Oviyu and the others in the car and stepped through the door and onto the crowded platform in the warm, humid air.

Having overslept and arrived late to the dining car for breakfast—most of the white-linen tables vacant and covered with plates of leftover food—Richard Boyle hurriedly ate as much as he felt time would allow, while glancing out the windows to the bright daylight where farms and the vegetation of the coast had replaced the barren plain. Gulping down the last of his coffee as the train entered the station, he stood and quickly made his way back to the compartment to retrieve his bag, as the porters continued to call out "*Mombasa—Mombasa*", and provide various last second assistance for the sleeper-car passengers.

*   *   *

"*Move—go! Move—go!*" Outside the decrepit doors of the sprawling Galaxy nightclub, in the heat and humidity of the midday sun, Benji walked with the crowd being pushed along by the two uniformed policemen who futilely attempted to show force and order in the people-clogged hotel and bar district. "*Move! Move!*" They pushed at some of the girls in their short skirts and painted lips, all with cheap, two-schilling rubber sandals on their feet, who either laughed or yelled angrily back as they grudgingly moved away from the doors. Even at this hour the sidewalk was packed with women, hundreds and hundreds, outnumbering males fifteen to one, feeding into the string of music-blasting bars that lined the street of two-story, humidity-stained buildings. Standing out like rabbits in a field of coal, the white-dressed foreign sailors pushed in and out of the doorways and down the crowded sidewalk, their hands gripping firmly the wallets buried deep within their pockets, hopelessly instructing the swarms of girls who surrounded and clutched at them like flies to meat to back away. Benji was suddenly knocked into the street by the crowd and turned just as two laughing, red-faced sailors brushed quickly past; and he looked into their eyes and saw the hyena spirit-of-the-dead fluttering around their pink, grinning faces.

The sailors were quickly gone and Benji looked up and saw what he had come to Moi Street to find: the Glory Guest House, where he hoped to find Constance and maybe Edgar, who had found the American sailor. Edgar had found him in Angie's room when he came in with the morning bucket of water, naked on the bed with the knife still stuck in his chest, staring wide-eyed at the ceiling, his prick rigid, but not from arousal, the young sailor not looking happy, like he had just been given unwelcome news. But then a ferocious storm of chaos had swept in as first the local then military police, with sirens blaring, arrested everyone in the building. They took all thirty of them to the basement of the municipal police station and conducted interrogations. And of those of whom it was sensed might know something worth knowing—or of whom there was simply a personal disdain—beatings. And now, six weeks later, according to the telegram from Ma Elizabeth, which had been awaiting Benji in Kijiado when he had returned from the mountain, Constance and Edgar were back at the Glory, back to the ancient daily routine of coastal Kenya.

In the municipal jail sat Angie, charged as an accomplice to the murder of Ensign Stuart McGrath.

*   *   *

"They aren't as interested as they were two days ago." Alice sat sideways on the car seat with the door open and her feet on the ground. Three of the lions had left and the other two had moved further up the riverbed, almost to where it curved out of sight.

Mark squatted on the ground beside his open door, having made a small pile of sticks and scraps of paper and a wadded-up *Standard* a short distance from the car. "If we had that one we could make a bonfire." He nodded toward a large tangled branch sticking out of the sand across the creek bed. Alice looked for a moment at the sun-bleached wood and then suddenly rose from her seat and walked around the front of the car and began to cross the creek bed.

"Alice!" Mark snapped. "—*Alice!*"

In the heat of the afternoon sun, she strode over to the protruding end and quickly freed it and began dragging it back across the sandy bottom. At the distant bend of the creek bed, still lying on the ground, the two lions turned their heads toward her.

"There," she said, reaching the car and throwing the branch to the ground beside the smaller pile; and she began breaking it up, pinning it to the ground with her foot and bending sections upward until they snapped, stopping when the thickness became too great.

"Here, let me try..." Mark leaned the fat end into the wheel well and struck with his foot until it cracked and snapped in two. "There." At the bend, the lions stood up and faced the car. Alice stared at them defiantly, and Mark, glancing once also, collected the new pile of debris and stacked it onto the rest, tripling the amount. On the backseat floor was the quarter-full bottle of kerosene left from the car camp and the box of matches. "It's not going to burn very long," Mark said. "We should spread it out."

"No. The bigger the better. It's the only way anyone might see it. Just before sundown—best chance for when anyone's heading back to a lodge. There's a lot of movement then, a plane might even be out."

"All right—" Mark looked at his watch. "In about an hour."

They got back in the car and Mark reached down

and handed the water bottle to Alice who unscrewed the top and took a small sip from the remaining inch. She handed it back and Mark took his and screwed the top back on. He looked at Alice for a moment and then pulled her over to him and she leaned silently against him in the warm afternoon air.

At the bend, still on their feet, the lions yawned and stretched, as though they too had plans for the evening.

*   *   *

Ann Boyle drove the Land Rover out of the parking lot at Rupert's, the new stuffed-elephant sideways in the backseat, it's trunk against the door, its big eyes staring out the window. Pulling back onto Uhura Highway and checking her watch, she accelerated into the late afternoon traffic, leaning forward once to better view her eyes in the rearview mirror, which showed the failure of the makeup to have improved the ever-darkening bags. With alternating glances between the road and the dashboard, she pushed in the cassette-tape protruding from the deck and began to adjust the volume and tone of the symphonic music which now came from the four car-speakers. Higher she turned the volume; and the Prague Symphony Orchestra first overwhelmed the noise of the engine and traffic, and then of her mind. Louder still, until it approached distortion, almost like a rock concert, but with the flowing harmony of strings and horns. Down the highway she sped, Mozart massaging her mind, toward the West Nairobi school where her wonderful Tobin would be coming out the doors in another ten minutes. They would have hamburgers for dinner tonight, she thought, cooked by Dominic, and potato chips, before taking the stuffed animal to Maggie. And later, games and TV.

*　　　*　　　*

At the end of the massive, still-being-constructed pier—barges with towering cranes driving in forms for concrete pilings—Richard Boyle crossed the metal walkway to the deck of the ship in the warm Indian Ocean breeze with the ensign who led him into the bowels and down to sickbay. He signed a sheet at the door and thanked the escort and spoke briefly with the attendant nurse who led him into the ward. Moving down the row of mostly vacant beds, they came to where Ensign Jimmy Hawkins lay, bandages covering his head, an I.V. in his arm, staring straight ahead, drowsy from painkillers. After an introduction and a few words with the patient, the nurse left and Richard stood at Hawkins side and touched his arm as their eyes met. "Tough few weeks, son?" Hawkins looked at Boyle then looked away. "Jimmy, I have some photographs I need you to look at. I want you to tell me if anyone looks familiar." He took an album from his briefcase and opened to a head-shot of a man and held it up to Hawkins. Almost immediately Hawkins shook his head, and Boyle turned the page. Again a head shake, and again, and then at the fourth, squinting, a nod. "How do you know him, Jimmy"? Boyle asked.

"He was with the girl."

Now Boyle flipped ahead to a female. "Her?" Hawkins nodded again. "Jimmy, we have to be very certain. I want you to look real closely.

Boyle flipped back to the man and again Hawkins squinted and again he nodded. "I'll never forget that face," he said, his voice weak and strained; and he gave a slight shrug and sighed and then looked away.

"Are you going home soon?"

"They aren't sure...I hope."

"I hope so, too." Boyle touched Hawkins arm again. "We'll find him, son. And he'll be put away. Stuart was a fine sailor. We'll find him for his family, for the Navy."

As soon as Richard reached his hotel and checked in, he called the hospital and they connected him to Maggie's room where Ann and Tobin were both with her. He spoke briefly with Ann who then put Maggie on the line.

"Hi Daddy."

"Hi sweetheart. How's the tummy today?"

"...Hurts."

"Is the tummy sore again?"

"Ah-huh...Daddy, will you be home tonight?"

"No, sweetheart. Daddy has to stay in Mombasa. Daddy will be home as soon as he can."

"...Oh."

"Daddy loves you, sweetheart. Daddy will be home soon."

"...I love you, Daddy."

*   *   *

When they heard the plane they both leaped from the car where they had been silently staring at the barren landscape and knelt at the wood pile where Mark poured from the kerosene bottle and Alice got the matches ready. The lions were no longer at the bend.

This plane, which had appeared suddenly from above the ridge to the east, seemed to be heading directly toward them. With the toss of the match, the pile exploded in a roar that momentarily drowned out the approaching engine before subsiding into a large, crackling fire, just moments before the plane was almost directly overhead. Now they grabbed the colored shirts they had tied together and began shouting and swinging wildly in the middle of the channel. They abruptly stopped when the plane disappeared above the eroded bluff, and listened, motionless, to the fading engine. It grew quieter, and quieter, until it was almost gone, and then seemed to stay the same; the faintest of low buzzes, and now seeming to move in a different direction. Then the sound of the plane began to grow.

"He's coming back. He's coming back!" Mark shouted, his now-bearded face adding to the wild look of his manic state. Alice glanced at him quickly then resumed her focus in the direction of the slowly growing drone. Now Mark suddenly kicked excitedly at the fire with its thin, barely-visible column of smoke, and a burst of sparks and flames shot high into the air.

"The leaves—throw the leaves on," Alice said anxiously, and Mark grabbed the small pile of brush and leaves they had been able to gather. Now the engine grew loud again and the plane suddenly appeared from beyond the bluff, a mile up the creek bed, and began to bank downstream toward them. They jumped wildly again, waving their arms and the shirt banners, shouting reflexively, as the smoke from the fire thickened. Only somewhat lower in altitude than its first passing, the plane crossed rapidly downstream opposite them, clearly in view, but beyond the detection of people in the windows, with no tilting of the wings or spurting of the engine, and just as quickly disappeared down the plain, slowly fading until the crackling of the fire again replaced the drone of the engine.

"He saw us. *He saw us!*" Mark shouted ecstatically. "We've been found! Someone... someone should be here...soon...real soon. Maybe tonight. If not tonight, tomorrow." He ran to Alice still holding one of the shirt-banners and wrapped his arms around her, briefly lifting her off the ground.

Alice gave him a small hug, but with an expression of concern, a weary expression that did not exude optimism. An expression that knew from a long history of sometimes crushing disappointments the insignificance and unimportance of her well being in life's grand scheme. "Why didn't he signal us?"

"He did. He came back!"

"Why hasn't he come back now, and signaled now? He could have been anyone. He could have been a poacher. He could have thought we were just camping. There's campers all over."

"We waved at him. He had to have seen us waving. —Christ, Alice, he saw us." Now the elation rapidly drained from Mark and turned to anger. "He saw us, Alice. He came back, he saw our fire, he saw us waving; he saw our car. *What more do you want?*"

Alice reached over with her arm and tried to smile. "All right. Let's get out of the sun. Someone should be here in the morning." Mark looked distantly at the fire which was almost out but still heavily smoking. Alice removed her arm and they walked back to the car.

*   *   *

"Bring the cassava, bring the pepper, bring them, bring them..." Ma Elizabeth spoke firmly in *Swahili* to Regina, her thirteen year old daughter, who went to the broken freezer in the corridor to bring more ingredients for the evening meal that Ma Elizabeth prepared at the counter. Two very young children played on the floor, attended to by eight-year old Audrey, another daughter, as various other women who lived or worked at the Glory Guest House sat on stools chopping food or stirring pots that simmered over small kerosene cookers. On a couch to the side, in shorts and short-sleeved shirts, Benji and Edgar sat below a single, hanging light bulb that illuminated the small, second-floor living quarters of the guest house.

Ma Elizabeth, wrapped in the loud, bright colors of her *Kangas* cloth—a matching scarf on her head and the large loops of earrings hanging from each lobe—took the pepper and peeled-cassava from Regina and threw them into separate pots, as she stirred a third pot with her other hand. Periodically, during her rapid movements, she placed small bits of leftovers into the mouth of an infant that bounced, facing her, on the knee of Constance, who held outward the babies short, fat arms. Rapid *Swahili* shot loudly back and forth between all four of the adults in the cramped room, which, along with being the kitchen and eating room, was what passed for an office and a living room, with a desk and the couch, and on a table, the radio-cassette deck with its detachable speakers.

"This man, Kenneth—bad man," Constance said

in *Swahili* to Benji and Edgar as she bounced the infant.

"Very bad," said Edgar, also in *Swahili*, who had been summoned from his home in another part of Mombasa when it was learned that Angie's brother had traveled from Kijiado. "Very violent. Oh, he drink and drink. But I believe she is no longer with him. She is with the sailor. She no longer wants Kenneth there. But he runs many of the girls. I saw him when I left late the night before. I had not seen him for some few weeks. But he was there out front, in the crowd, standing."

"They say he is still in Mombasa, he has been seen," said Constance, the baby's beaming face searching for its mother as it bounced on her knee. "He is owing to this clan—the *Shela*. They will know if he tries to go." She furrowed her brow: "It is they who bring the girls here—some form *Uganda-land!*" She looked at Benji. "I cry and cry. The police, they keep Angie because they think she is with Kenneth. The sailor is in her room. The American. She has become friends with him. More. They take us all to headquarters. Beatings. Even Ma Elizabeth they arrest—*who is to take care of all these children?*"

"Two days!" Ma Elizabeth said loudly in *Swahili* as she stirred and chopped. "The hotel is overrun upon return: people, people, people... These Kenyans. Oh, Allah, I'm telling you." She stuck another piece of food in the baby's mouth and wiped away the drool.

*   *   *

Angie stared at the bare tabletop, seated across from Benji, the two Kenyan policemen standing by the door. At two other tables in the brightly-lit jail room, several other people engaged in subdued conversation.

"He is here... He is here... It is all I know," Angie said in *Maa-Irusa*, more loudly than the barely audible voice she had been using since her brother had been brought into the room, her eyes still moist.

Benji, searching for clues to Kenneth's whereabouts, struggled to mask his sorrow at the sight of his incarcerated sister, and anger at the path she had followed—or been led down. He had just begun climbing the mountain when Kenneth first appeared in Kijiado, more than a year before, selling his foolish shirts, and sweeping Angie off her feet. Angie—who had not fully recovered from her failed exams at the regional Secondary School, which kept her from the elite college in Nairobi, growing increasingly restless in Kijiado, not wanting to marry the second son of their mother's third brother, who someday would become Chief of the *Eleyo*—leaving suddenly with Kenneth. The mountain, with its swarms of wealthy foreigners marching obsessively up to the snowfields, raining more money onto the landscape than all the maize that had ever been grown and sold in Kijiado since Nga'i had made the plains, keeping Benji away for months at a time. He had *manamba,* the other porters told him with wide grins; he put the travelers to the dark continent at ease; they tipped him big.

Now, in the dank jail room, Angie began to talk.

"I was no longer with Kenneth. Not for a long time. —Oh, he drinks and drinks. But I loved Stuart. *Yeye anaipenda! He loved me!* He wants me for a wife—he would have taken me to America!" She brought the handkerchief to her eyes again. "Kenneth became jealous. By now he is big man for these sailors—but only because of the *Shela.* They make him big. Ship after ship. In they come. They want girls. Kenneth gives girls. They stop on the way north. They stop on the way back. Now they know the girls..." She turned away from her brother. "Yes, I sleep with Stuart. He takes care of me. Sends me money. Loves me. I no longer want Kenneth. Stuart, and his friend—this boy, Jimmy—one night they chase him out. Then Stuart gets assigned to port so he can stay with me, all of time. Then Constance's mother is sick—for two weeks, the fever—so together we go to Malindi, to help. When I come back... Stuart is dead...the boy hurt bad. Everyone in jail. They take me. First they think I kill Stuart. Then they think Kenneth. They know I come to Mombasa with him. They think I know where he hides, that I protect him." She looked pleadingly at Benji. "This man, Boyle, he is only one who believes. He has gone back to Nairobi. He say he will come back...but now, four weeks..." At first she cried softly, then reaching across to her brother, began to sob.

*   *   *

Under the brilliant morning sun, the beige mini-van pulled through the gate of Nairobi National Park on the outskirts of the city and wound the short distance through the sparse forest to the animal orphanage and stopped at the small visitors building.

The three adults and four children piled out onto the dusty ground and Ann and Rosanne unfolded the wheelchair and lifted Maggie from the van and into the chair. With an excited yet obedient buzz, the children hovered around Maggie as Tobin pushed the chair up the ramp and through the entrance to where donations were made and warm greetings exchanged with Karl, the on-duty Kenyan attendant, who bent down with a wide smile to hug his dear and familiar friend. And below the scarf that covered her hairless scalp, Maggie's small, pale face, upon seeing her loving Karl, beamed the brightest yet of the morning.

As the excited chatter of the children grew, Karl spoke briefly to Ann about Doevee, and how the elephant was progressing well and should be ready for release within a few months, and then he asked about Maggie. And in a softer voice Ann briefly spoke with him more, and then with Tobin continuing to push his sister, and the others following, Karl led everyone out the back and into the open-air sanctuary which was crossed with several waist-high fences, first passing a small, juvenile rhinoceros resting on the muddy ground amongst piles of hay beside a water trough. Now the children periodically darted ahead to the edges of various pens, both empty and occupied, until everyone eventually came to a gate, beyond which, facing them in the leafy-shade of a tall Eucalyptus tree in the half-acre pen, stood a small elephant. Now Maggie's eyes opened from the near slits they had previously been, until they were wider than those of any of the others; and she stared straight at Doevee as Tobin pushed the chair across the dirt to where Doevee stood. With the adults and children now gathered silently around, Karl gently reached over and caressed the rough hide of the trunk which the young pachyderm slowly raised into the air. As he continued the gentle caresses, he spoke softly in *Bantu* and brought Doevee a step closer as Maggie, pale and silent in her powdery blue dress and scarf, raised her arms upward; and the curving trunk slowly lowered and extended out to the girl's hands and gently encircled them.

*   *   *

On Moi street in Mombasa, between the Galaxy and Zanze nightclubs on one side, and the Twiga, Gypsy, and Star on the other, there were hundreds and hundreds of sailors, jammed in amongst the hundreds and hundreds of women, filling every table and square foot of floor space and spilling out the doorways and flooding the sidewalks and streets. Most of the sailors clasping bottles of Tusker or Guiness, or shot-glasses of spirits, standing, sitting, leaning, or, when they could force room in the space between the tables, dancing wildly with a partner. All of them drunk and loud, which, along with the blaring of the bar stereos and the high chatter of the women, created a near roar of sound.

Benji pushed through the crowd across the floor of the Galaxy with Edgar and Constance, Constance searching the faces flashing before her, greeting and questioning those she knew, seeking Kenneth's whereabouts, all of the women touching her arm, asking with deep concern about Angie. With the second aircraft carrier having docked that afternoon, along with its three support ships, the crowd was as large as Constance, a Moi street veteran of more than three years, had ever seen: the highly-trained first-world, war-technicians ashore at the exotic African port; standing on the dark continent. Like a ride at an amusement park: take the *Enterprise* to Africa, leave only your money and sperm. And all of Mombasa descended on them, waiting at the pier gate for the dam to burst and unleash the flood of currency that would pour into the city; until three days later when the enormous steel fortresses slipped back out amongst the crisscrossing sails of the wood-flotilla of

Arab-dhows plying the harbor waters as they had for the past thousand years.

"*Constance! Constance!* He is here. He got Mellisa. This morning. The Tana." In the middle of the packed Galaxy crowd, the girl with the frightened, distant look grasped both of Constances' hands and spoke tearfully in *Swahili* of the beating of her sister, Mellisa, that morning at the Tana Hotel. All of the girls of the *Glory* had known to report Kenneth's whereabouts to Ma Elizabeth and to avoid him at all costs. But when Mellisa disappeared a few days before, they feared she may have gone with him, and when they found her battered and barely conscious at the Tana, they knew she had. Kenneth was at the Tana, broke and desperate, hunted by a *Swahili* clan, hunted by the police, hunted by the Glory.

"Okay. Okay," said Constance amongst the blasting of the music and the roar of the crowd, consoling and thanking the woman, before turning to Benji and Edgar. "The Tana," she said in *Irusa*, "he has been seen this morning. We must find Mr. Boyle. Police Headquarters. We must hurry."

They found Kenneth a few hours later in the alley behind the *Tana,* under a scrap-sheet of corrugated tin in a stairwell leading to the cellar. The six military police from the ship, led by Boyle, and the twelve Mombasa police, surrounding the area, storming into the building from the front and rear, pistols drawn, shouts and threats quickly eliciting the desired information from all the startled and terrified occupants encountered within. The Mombasian police who found him first, dragging him out form under the tin and briefly beating him, before Boyle and the M.P.s intervened and led him away.

They let Angie go the next day, Boyle securing her release, convinced from interviews with Constance and Mellisa and Ma Elizabeth that she was not a participant, then, after securing sufficient funds, convincing the head detective of the Mombasa Police Force. She would have to return in a month for the trial, but before the day was over, she and Benji were at the train station. And carrying their bags and with her brother's arm around her, they boarded the Nairobi sleeper for the return home to Kijiado.

*   *   *

Alice lay across the back seat of the Corolla in the warm afternoon air, windows down, knees bent, staring at the ceiling. Across the front lay Mark. Her lips badly parched, she looked at her watch, knowing before hand that it would say 1:50, having last looked at it ten minutes before, and ten minutes before that. "They aren't coming. You might as well face it," she said softly but firmly. Beside her was a bottle filled with several inches of her urine.

Mark stared silently at the ceiling. The plastic quart water-bottle lay empty on the floor. Beside it stood another bottle with several inches of his urine. Alice slowly sat up, the bottle in her hand, and scanned the barren landscape below the overcast sky.

It had been cloudy since the sun came up and the mountain was gone. They had heard distant thunder throughout much of the sleepless night, waiting for daylight to come, when the rescuers would surely appear. They had also heard the lions, and what they guessed were hyenas, louder and nearer than in previous nights. At one point, during a period of quiet, Mark had suddenly jumped up and shouted that he heard a siren, the wailing 'hee-haw' 'hee-haw' of a European rescue vehicle. But after rapidly lowering the windows and a period of intense listening, and hearing only the wind, decided he was wrong. Shining out the window into the darkness what was left of the flashlight, it reflected back two sets of widely spaced eyes toward the brush where the lions had been.

But there were no lions in the morning; just the sudden streak of several impala darting across the creek bed in front of the car and up over the opposite bank. They had gotten out of the vehicle at the first sign of daylight and climbed to the top of the bluff. There the plain stretched into the distance for as far as they could see, the flat, dry, mud-cracked bottom of Lake Amboselli encompassing much of the view. Despite the web of dirt tracks, there were no towns or highways within walking distance in that direction, the barren, intensely-exposed plain eventually turning into the immense Serengeti.

"Didn't Benji say he had once walked across the lake bed?" Alice had asked as they stood at the top of the bluff in the early morning light.

"*Are you serious?*" Mark said incredulously.

"No—no...I wasn't...it was when he was young. He was telling us about it the night before the summit—I think you had gone to your tent. A truck or something had broken down. He was with his father, and a sister—I think he has a sister. Yeah, for some reason Peter told us not to ask about her... But they had to walk across part of the lake bed, like for a couple of days. They had plenty of water, and a hunting gun, but he said it was very difficult. He said he thinks about it the day before every summit climb."

Mark, scanning the barren plain, hadn't responded to the story, and with no sign of people, they soon climbed back down the bluff.

Sitting in the backseat in the warm afternoon air, looking out at the empty landscape, Alice drummed her fingers against the car top while shooting glances at her watch. "Mark, they aren't coming. You know that. I know you know that...Mark?"

Across the front seat, Mark continued to stare at the ceiling.

*　　*　　*

They were all gathered around Maggie at the hospital when she left. Ann and Richard and Tobin, Margaret and Frank, Alan and Rosanne, Dr.Sanger and Dr. Mygotta, the nurses and orderlies, all crowded into the large, softly-lit room, speaking quietly amongst themselves from time to time. She left with the stuffed elephant beside her, her small arm around the fuzzy neck, her mother and father leaning over from chairs beside her, caressing her soft skin, telling her it was all right, they loved her, they would always love her, and it was all right. There was a small smile just before she stopped breathing, a moment after her eyes last looked into her mother's, then looked away, then a small smile.

Everyone stood silent and motionless for a moment, then with a nod from Ann, quietly left the room, the last, Rosanne, gently closing the door; and Ann and Richard, hands still caressing their daughter, blinked futilely at the tears that streamed down their faces.

*　　*　　*

"Angie! Angie!" The elderly Kenyan woman, running with outstretched arms from the entrance of the small mud and cement-block farmhouse on the edge of Kijiado, called out elatedly to the son and daughter approaching from the dirt road.

"*Ma-ma! Ma-ma!*" Angie began to run toward her mother, arms also extended, grinning widely, as Benji, also with a smile, carried the bags across the yard. From the house came an elderly man, his weathered face squinting out at the commotion before him, then he too bursting into elation when he recognized his daughter, and rushing forward as quickly as his old, tired legs would carry him.

"*Oh, my baby! My baby!*" the woman sobbed in *Irusa* as she reached and embraced Angie, who squeezed back with all the strength she had.

Now others emerged from the house—a young man and woman and several children and adolescents—and also came excitedly down to the embracing group; and, moments later, under the overcast sky, they all slowly made their way back up to the house.

*   *   *

"Let's go, Mark."

"Alice—no."

"You aren't going to make it through the night here, Mark. We've got to go."

"Alice..."

With her feet on the ground out the open back door, she glanced briefly at the barren scrub. "Mark, I'm going. Right now. While I still have some strength."

"Alice...you know what's out there..."

She leaned over and tightened the laces of her hiking-boots, then stuck the urine bottle in her day pack and placed the full-brimmed hat onto her head.

"Alice...what are you doing? Alice...don't..."

She stood up and closed the door and walked around to the driver's window. She was grinning. "This is the perfect time. Look...clouds."

"Alice..."

"You really should come, Mark... But look, try to make it through the night. I'll be back in the morning." She leaned in through his open window and gave him a quick kiss on the forehead.

"Alice!..."

She stared at him for a moment, gave another quick grin, and threw on the day pack. "I got a date with King Tut, honey." She winked and headed across the creek bed.

*   *   *

"Ngotu, the piss-blood is from Gory's oxen. You leave your wife's gourds by the fuga bush where they like to piss."

"Ntela, smell the blood, this is Mbola's boy, Dubani. He takes the sumba gourds to Koya's house and leaves them by that old goat. Taste this—Koya's goat-piss! Here, drink the fresh blood."

Squatting in the shade of the tree beside several grazing cattle at the edge of the thorn-encircled manyatta-camp, the tall Masai herder—sandaled and red-shaka robed—raised the slender gourd of blood and milk to his lips in the warm, late-afternoon air. He took several gulps, then smiled as he lowered the gourd, and continued speaking in Maa-Matapo. "Ah, Ngotu, it is good. But don't let my wife see—she is just there, beyond Keta's house." Now the herder looked with concern at his friend. "Ngotu, she wants to fornicate again tomorrow morning. The Laibon has told her to take my seed before the sun reaches Ngái-Kahn. He says then she will bear a daughter whose heart will beat. Ngái has given us all boys—very fine for me—for the death of my wife's Queen Mother four lives ago. She has to have a daughter, Ngotu—she tells me every night—to ease the burden of her work. ...It is why I am not to drink milk from Ndeles cattle."

Ngotu smiled widely and abruptly laughed. "Ah! Ntela! Can Ngái laugh louder? He plays with your wife. Seven boys—no girl for her!" He drank again from the first gourd, briefly staring at it. "Ah, Ntela, you know, it is Koya's goat piss—here."

"Okay—a little more."

Ngotu's expression momentarily turned serious and he looked again at his friend. "But, Ntela, you know you will not be fornicating when the sun next rises—not in your bed!" He grinned widely and laughed again. "The rains...Olopiro, Ntela. Tonight, Olopiro kali!"

Now Ntela grew animated. "Ngotu, I tell my wife. She knows Olopiro comes tonight! But she drinks little Forya's cunt-blood all week! —Have you not smelled her? I tell her we will all be learning to swim when the sun next visits. But, no! The Laibon has instructed her to Kima's house—on the hill! There, after the rains, Nseea will visit her womb. I am to give the seed. If Nseea is happy with the cattle I have paid the Laibon, the daughter's spirit will be there!"

"Ah, Ntela, yours are good cattle. Nseea will be pleased. Here, drink more, your wife has gone into Keta's home. They are busy. All are preparing for Olopiro. Look, here come our boys now. Oh, Ntela, see the sky. It is time to move these cattle to the hill."

*   *   *

It was pitch black when it began to rain. Pitch black and then bright as day when the lightning flashed. At first the rain fell in sheets. Then with the wind came the deluge; and the skies emptied in a torrent.

In the car, pressed against the driver's door, Mark turned his head toward the rolled-down window and opened his mouth as the rain battered his blistered face. He reached over and pulled the door handle and tumbled to the ground, landing on his back and facing the sky, and tried to swallow the rain. He rolled onto his knees and found the plate and cooking pot they had kept under the car for this very reason and held them up to the falling water. As the pot began to fill, he tipped the film of moisture already on the plate into his mouth and felt the few drops pass into his throat.

Now he felt moisture near his knees and during the flashes of lightning saw the growing rivulet that was flowing beside the car. At first it was just a few inches wide, but it quickly expanded to a foot, and then two; and struggling to his feet he sprawled over the hood of the car. As the thunder cracked and the lightning illuminated everything around him, the wind, now howling, began violently swaying the branches of the trees lining the bluff. Then from up the creek bed he heard the rushing swirl. At first it sounded like an approaching truck, or a train, and then like a large wave; and he had only the briefest of moments before it struck him and the car and sent him crashing against the door. As the flood roared against him, he quickly grabbed hold of the back door handle but let go when the car began to lift and turn. He floated for a moment before striking the protruding trunk of a fallen tree leaning over from the bank and held on for dear life as the car, rolling over onto its top, headed down the roaring creek. He held on for another moment, and held on and held on, until he could hold on no more, and then he let go.

*   *   *

(One month later)

"The plain is waiting for you. Your family is here. Your mother, the earth, has filled all your plates and gourds with the favorite foods of one of her children. She has been waiting for you to come home." Karl stood beside the small elephant, speaking softly in Bantu, as the driver and the assistant stood back by the truck and the short ramp leading from the empty trailer to the dirt of the remote track road. In the distance, like swaying gray bumps protruding from the barren ground, a herd of elephants moved slowly across the plain.

With a sharp swat of the stick he held in his hand, Karl struck once at the eye-level rear of the creature, and with raised trunk and trumpet-like calls, it bolted into the short scrub, moving in rapid zigzags out across the plain. Karl watched as it momentarily disappeared into a shallow ravine and then reappeared on the other side and continued in a trot toward the distant, slow-moving herd. He watched for another moment, then turned back to the truck as the assistant loaded the ramp and closed the trailer door and the driver started the engine. He turned and looked one last time at the distant trail of dust, then climbed into the truck.

Amongst the short scrub, the elephant slowed its trot to a walk and stopped, alone on the plain, the herd still in the distance. It raised its trunk into the air and turned it from side to side, the nostrils flaring and contracting. It moved forward a few more steps and slowly lowered its trunk to the ground where a small, torn, day pack lay, and gently pushed against the object. It stood motionless for a moment, lightly sniffing back and forth over the surface of the material, slightly moving it on the ground. Then, raising its trunk back into the air and snorting once, it abruptly turned, and headed swiftly again toward the herd, on the wide African plain.

About the Author

Rick Fordyce taught high school math and English for two years in the late 1970s with the Peace Corps in Ghana, West Africa. He is the author of several works of fiction. He lives in Seattle and Cape Cod.